To MUAH
-Alea
MW01118344

CLOUD FILLY

By Alea Bushardt

Illustrated By Jeanne Mellin

Edited By Melody Clayton

© Copyright 2006 Alea Bushardt.

All rights reserved. No part of this publication may be reproduced, stored in a retrieval system, or transmitted, in any form or by any means, electronic, mechanical, photocopying, recording, or otherwise, without the written prior permission of the author.

www.sunridgepress.com

Note for Librarians: A cataloguing record for this book is available from Library and Archives Canada at www.collectionscanada.ca/amicus/index-e.html

ISBN 1-4120-5429-X

Printed in Victoria, BC, Canada. Printed on paper with minimum 30% recycled fibre.
Trafford's print shop runs on "green energy" from solar, wind and other environmentally-friendly power sources.

Offices in Canada, USA, Ireland and UK

Book sales for North America and international:
Trafford Publishing, 6E–2333 Government St.,
Victoria, BC V8T 4P4 CANADA
phone 250 383 6864 (toll-free 1 888 232 4444)
fax 250 383 6804; email to orders@trafford.com

Book sales in Europe:
Trafford Publishing (UK) Limited, 9 Park End Street, 2nd Floor
Oxford, UK OX1 1HH UNITED KINGDOM
phone 44 (0)1865 722 113 (local rate 0845 230 9601)
facsimile 44 (0)1865 722 868; info.uk@trafford.com

Order online at:
trafford.com/05-0325

10 9 8 7 6 5 4 3 2 1

Thanks to

Annie
For letting me really learn how to ride

Laura
For giving me something to look forward to

Magnum
For being my wild racehorse and
inspiring me to do crazy things

My laptop
For saving my book instead of deleting it,
even when I called you a #@$%!!!!

My Mom
For everything

Greetings, reader!

The book you are reading this from took a little over a year to finish. It is ten chapters long and I forgot how many pages. It has sucked dry the author's 14 year old peanut brain.

Not to worry, though (unless you end up hating this book and want to burn it or something)! This is hopefully the first in a few. As you read this, the author has finished the sequel and is hard at work on the following one. It will pick up where this one and the next one leaves off, so hopefully they will come together and make sense properly.

If this book seems a little childish to you, it's because the idea was made up when I was seven. The storylines have gone from being drawings, to comic strips, to short stories, and now finally a book. Of course, I have made certain modifications and made it as mature as I think it's going to get. Detailing in depth is hard when there were no scientific explanations for anything in the first place.

I have loved my scribblings of stories since I first came up with them, and I hope there are at least some out there who would also. I like to write all the time, for the good fun of it, as many other teens my age who like writing do, and I have many other characters besides the ones in this book who somehow will hopefully make it into publishing one day. There is an endless blooper reel on these books. Maybe that, too, will be published one day.

And the last warning: this isn't the best literature you will ever read. I apologize if I have made mistakes in here. I did the best I could and I will hopefully get better as I write more. Now, if you want great horse books read the Silver Brumby or The Black Stallion series, and let's not forget Smoky the Cowhorse. But, if you want oddness, randomness, and horsey/unicorny books with lots of made up words and strange situations, then go no further!

Much love and happy reading!

~Alea

Contents

Chapter 1

Drake's Dream

Twelve thoroughbreds exploded onto the track. Hooves digging into the dirt, nostrils flared, slicing through the hot air, horses of all shades of brown and black through steely gray thundered down the stretch. A great bay took the lead, slicing into the earth with sharp hooves, then tossing the dirt out behind him in his haste to leave the field behind. But he could not, because the small jockey on his back was pulling back on his mouth, and holding him steady so he would not run himself into the ground.

The track announcer called the positions of the horses, and it hardly seemed any time at all until the horses came flying down the backstretch towards the finish line. The big bay in front faded back, and a nearly black colt suddenly emerged from the back of the pack, leaving the other horses behind. He was a blur crossing the finish line, winner by two lengths.

Fifteen year old, brown haired Drake cheered like it was New Years, though he couldn't see who had won. He was watching the race (or part of it) from a tall tree next to the grandstand. He had no money to buy tickets. Still, he came to watch races almost every day.

"I told you he would win," said his younger sister, Nellie, who was sitting up at the very top of the tree. "The black one won." She smiled at him slyly.

"How do I know you're not just saying that because I can't see the finish line?" Drake replied.

Both of them climbed down the tree, and onto the grass. They had been watching most of the day, and making silent bets on who would win.

"You always pick the black horses," Drake said as they walked.

"Well, you always pick the grays and chestnuts!" Nellie replied, tossing her black curls in a defiant sort of way.

Drake didn't hear her. Now he was deep in thought. The day he turned sixteen, he was going to get a jockey license, then become the youngest jockey ever to win the Kentucky Derby! Who cared if he had never ridden a horse before?

"Drake? Drake?" Nellie said, waving her hand in front of her practically drooling brother's face. She shook her head. "You and your jockey dreams."

"Hey!" Drake said, snapping out of it at this. "It could happen!" He got a dreamy look on his face again. "And I'll be riding a flaming red colt, and we'll beat old Will O the Wisp's world record by an entire second, too."

Nellie gave him a look. "That's crazy talk. Wisp was the greatest racehorse there ever was. There will never be another one like him, I'm sure of that. What makes you think you could beat him?"

The two argued all the way home. Or, at least, Nellie tried to argue while Drake dreamed about the Run for the Roses. They lived in a small house with their mom, dad, and six brothers and sisters. It was very crowded, and Drake couldn't wait to get out of there. Then he could buy his own horse and jockey it himself. He had always wanted a horse, but they had been too poor to own one. Besides, his mother thought they were a pointless animal nowadays, and loved only by "Those with much money." But all Drake wanted was a horse to race, show, or even just trail ride. He had even tried to buy a donkey once. (The deal fell through when his mom caught him at the last moment. He cried for a week.)

They came to their home and went inside. It was hot and uncomfortable, because their air conditioner was broken. It had actually been for quite a while. When he was a millionaire jockey, he would have to remember to send money home.

Two of Drake's younger siblings scampered by, followed

by a third who was running blindly with a pot on his head. Drake's mother, who was middle aged with dark, wavy hair, peered out of the living room and greeted them with a tired "How was your day?"

"High school was normal, but afterwards we went and saw some more horse races," Drake said. "Say, can I have an allowance so we won't have to sit in the tree and we can actually see the entire race?"

Mother gave a weary sigh. "I would love to give you the money, but we just can't afford it right now. The dress ended up costing more than I thought it would."

Drake knew she was referring to the beautiful yellow dress Nellie was wearing. It was one of the few fancy clothes they had. Nellie adored the dress, though she tried not to show it too much. She wanted to keep at least a little 'tough girl' exterior… and she didn't want her mother to think she felt bad she only had the one.

Nellie looked at her feet. "I don't really need the dress anymore. You could sell it if you wanted."

"No, you look the prettiest in it." Her mother replied, a small sparkle in her eyes. "I couldn't bear to see it on some pale, overweight child."

Nellie smiled and quickly turned to go to her room. Drake decided to do the same, until dinnertime when their father would come home. He shared his room with three other brothers, so he only got a small bed in the corner. But his side was easy to recognize, since the walls were covered with posters of racehorses, and somewhere in there, under them, was one of a flying lemur.

Drake liked to dream, and it showed in his grades. Teachers called him unintelligent, but when it came to horse racing, Drake was an expert. He could easily recite the winners of the Kentucky Derby over the past few years, and their times. His very favorite racehorse was the greatest one, Will O the Wisp. The great dark stallion still held the Kentucky Derby track record, even though he raced in the 60's and it was now a new millennium. Everybody who knew about horse racing called him the greatest, and thought there would never be another like him. Drake was out to prove them wrong. Someday...

Drake stared absentmindedly at a poster of a gray racehorse. Then someone waved their hand in front of his face. He turned to see one of his little brothers staring at him curiously.

"Huh?"

"Can you drive a car?" The brother asked incredulously.

"No. I wish."

"Why is your hair brown?" He continued.

"Go away, Jeremy!"

Jeremy crossed his eyes at him and then ran out of the room pretending to be a jet plane. Drake searched for his book bag, then realized with dismay that he had left it in the tree at the racetrack. It would take him half an hour to get there, and half an hour to get back. It was already dark. Drake would have to get it the next morning, making him late for school.

Not like he minded.

"Shitake mushrooms!" Drake heard from next door. Apparently Nellie had done the same thing.

There was then the sound of a door opening and a chorus of "Daddy!" Drake came out of his room. Since their dad was home it was dinnertime. They were having... what else... TV dinners!

Drake sat next to Nellie at the table, and attempted to eat the TV dinner, but it was still frozen, so of course that didn't work. So, after 20 minutes of children fighting over the microwave Drake finally got to eat his Salisbury steak meal which took him hardly any time at all.

The next morning on the way to the track to find their book

bags they discussed the matter of when they could leave home.

"I'm going to leave the first chance I get," Nellie said. She was wearing the yellow dress again.

"Living in that little house is getting old, isn't it?" Drake agreed.

The track was bustling with horses and people, exercising and getting ready for races. Luckily no one was hanging around at the tree. Sure enough, there were their backpacks, sitting on high branches. They climbed up and got their stuff easily. Then Drake noticed a hole in the tree he had never seen before. It was up a little higher, but not so high that the limbs would break if he climbed up and looked in.

He looked closer. The hole had a strange sort of presence around it. Drake wanted to investigate.

"Hey Nellie! Look at this hole!"

Nellie looked at Drake in confusion. A hole. That seemed like nothing to be excited about. But Drake was climbing higher to look in. Typical Drake...

"I bet some squirrel is going to have a heart attack and scratch your eyes out if you poke your head in there!" she warned.

Drake ignored her and looked in cautiously. The tree was

hollow until a little way down, and then there was dark dirt. Drake poked his head in and looked down.

Suddenly, sounding odd due to his head being in the hole, Drake said "Nellie! You won't believe what's in here! Come help me get it!"

Nellie blinked and quickly climbed up after him. Drake waited for her, then pointed into the tree. She peered in. And she saw, resting in a bed of leaves, a glass orb. It was very clear, like glass, but it seemed to shine every color of the rainbow.

"Jackpot!" Drake whooped. Someone down below who was walking a horse looked up at him strangely before the horse noticed them so high and sidestepped warily. Nellie stared.

"Well don't just sit there, we have to get it! Just think what mom will say!" Drake said urgently.

"Well, what if someone is hiding it here?" Nellie asked, not moving a muscle.

"Well who would be hiding it here, garden gnomes?" Drake scoffed.

He reached down to try and get it but he couldn't reach it. "Nellie, help me here!"

Nellie grabbed his ankles and he dropped down. He almost had it. Almost... he could nearly touch it. Ah!

Then suddenly the world was a rush around him and Nellie. They were spinning like crazy, and the orb – the tree, the track – was nowhere in sight. They felt the sickening sensation of falling, and quickly. Nellie screamed.

The color whipping quickly across their vision was brilliant, and then it turned black, and then orange, and then multicolored again. Drake was spinning so fast he thought he was gonna puke. Just like he did that one time on the airplane – suddenly, they heard a deafening BANG, and they slammed into green grass.

"Hello? Are you alive? Helloooo?"

Drake opened his eyes groggily.

"...Ok...?"

Then he remembered the odd spinning deal, and as soon as his vision cleared he saw a purple – haired girl looking a bit older than Nellie leaning over him.

"I'm fine, we just fell out of the tree, that's aaaaa..." he managed to say quickly. Moving his head, he looked around. Wait. This was NOT the racetrack.

"AAAAAAAAAAAAAAH!" Nellie screamed beside him.

Drake had a very small moment to think sarcastically, *girls... gosh... ow, my ear...*

The purple – haired girl looked at them strangely. "You act like you've never used a portal before." She said in a simple voice.

"A WHAT?!" Drake screeched.

"A portal. See, now you're in Uni."

Drake looked beyond the purple – haired girl and saw that they were in a forest. Actually, it was pretty well kept for a forest. The only trees were tall, gray ones, and if you looked far enough past them on one side you could see emerald green plains of tall grass stretching for miles. To the side, the plains came quicker, with very few trees in the way, so they must've been at an edge of the forest. Directly behind the purple – haired girl there was a small house. It was made of gray logs. And peeking around the side of the house was a horse. But it wasn't a horse. It had a long, black horn on its forehead. Drake pinched himself.

This had to be a dream. "Nellie. Pinch me."

Nellie pinched him.

"Ow."

Nellie pinched him again. Then she did it again just for the fun.

"Ow. Ow! Okay so I'm not dreaming."

The purple-haired girl helped them both up.

"Where are you from?"

"Kentucky. What happened?"

"You must have touched a portal, because this is Uni…"

"What?" Drake interrupted at 'Uni'.

"Uni." She repeated, raising her eyebrows (which were also purple.)

Drake just looked at her. Nellie did the same.

"Uni!" she said again, sighing. "Don't tell me you've never been here. I'll have to pity you." She smiled at them.

"Uni… as in what?" This time, Nellie asked.

"Uni as in unicorn. Like him," she pointed quickly to the horse behind the house. "You know?"

Drake's eyes got quite round as he followed her gesture. "No way. Quit joking. There are no such things as unicorns."

The horse that was behind the house seemed to take this as a cue to walk up. It's coat was a golden color, accompanied by a black mane and tail and black lower legs. The horn on its forehead was black and shiny, and it peered at them with humanlike jade green eyes.

"Ah HA! Unicorns are white! This is obviously a fake," Drake said, coming up quickly and grabbing the poor horse's horn and tugging on it. It didn't come off. "Hey! Did you superglue a knick knack onto your horse's head?"

"Lemme see it." Nellie went over to the horse. It eyed her warily, its weight shifting back. She examined the horn, which really actually and truly seemed too be growing out of the horse's head.

"Quit messing with him!" the purple-haired girl cut in, sounding annoyed. "He's as real a unicorn as ever, and I'd never superglue anything to a horse!"

Drake looked down perceptively and pointed to the horse's shoes. They were definitely glued on.

"Well, I don't believe in driving nails through my unicorn's hooves, either." Then, both she and the unicorn nodded. "That's right." they said in unison. A small smile came on *both* their faces.

Drake and Nellie gawked. The horse/unicorn had talked!

Chapter 2

Magicalness!

"My name is Lorelei, and this is my unicorn friend, Alidar."
The purple haired girl said.

"Hi," Alidar said nervously.

Drake and Nellie gawked.

"The horse is talking. How is the horse talking?" Drake
thought out loud.

"Unicorns learn how to talk by listening to their owners." Lorelei supplied to his unintended question.

Nellie was still standing close, so she poked Alidar. He shrunk back. Lorelei put an arm in front of him protectively. "Quit messin' with my unicorn!" she said again.

"Sorry." Nellie couldn't take her eyes off of him. "I've never seen a talking horse – err, unicorn before."

Drake could only stare at the unicorn and Lorelei. Lorelei was wearing a long black dress, and her hair was a bit puffy and wild. Not looking like it was too easy to brush, either.

"Are you a witch?" He asked. Well hey, if there was a unicorn involved, why not?

Lorelei looked offended. "No. I'm a sorceress. I just like to wear black."

Drake shifted his weight away a little from her.

"Is that how you got your hair purple? By using some sort of spell or something?" Nellie asked, interrupting the silence.

"Yep," Lorelei said proudly. Then she pulled a stick – Drake, getting into this magical stuff now, figured it had to be a wand – out of her sleeve and pointed it at her hair. She chanted something short and sweet, and her hair turned orange.

Drake and Nellie gawked.

Then Lorelei pointed her wand at Drake and chanted something. He winced.

Nothing happened.

Then Nellie burst out laughing.

"Your hair... your hair... it's pink!"

Drake screeched, his hands flying up to touch it. "Change it back, change it back!!"

Lorelei once again pointed her wand at Drake and chanted something undecipherable. Drake felt his hair get heavy. Nellie nearly fell over laughing.

"Rainbow afro!! Rainbow afro!!"

Drake felt his hair some more. Maybe, if he played along, they'd stop. *Girls!* "Now if you could just turn it black...."

Lorelei laughed and changed his hair back to short and brown. Drake was about to ask an estimated forty three questions, when he saw another girl come out of the little house. She was wearing jeans. Ah, good, there were jeans here in Uni or whatever... she also had a black halter top, and had two long, beautiful golden blonde ponytails curving down her back. *Whoa*, Drake thought.

"Alidar," she called. Alidar gladly turned and trotted over to her, and she placed her hands on his withers and jumped onto his back even before he came to a full stop. Then she noticed Drake and Nellie. "Lorelei! Who's that?"

Lorelei pointed at Drake and Nellie.

"Drake," supplied Drake.

"Nellie," said Nellie.

"A Drake is a male duck," the blonde said, looking at them with neither high interest nor dislike.

Drake sighed, annoyed. At least they had familiar animals here.

"Oh, I guess I'd better introduce myself. I'm Valerie, Lorelei's, sorceress-in-training sister."

She pulled a wand similar to Lorelei's from her pocket. "I know a few spells and charms already."

Drake shrank back.

"Watch out! Blonde with a wand!" Nellie said, looking at Drake. Lorelei laughed.

The blonde rolled her eyes. "Rrrrgh…"

Valerie turned Alidar, the little stallion seeming to know where to go just by where she looked, and gunned him into a fast canter off to the plains. "I'll see you later," she called as she disappeared behind a hill.

Lorelei shook her head. "That girl is too cocky for her own good. And she's stealing my unicorn!"

"She wasn't that bad," Drake said thoughtfully.

"Well, do you want to come in?"

They looked at one another, and soon all went into

Lorelei's house, which was crowded and small. The windows and doors were all open, letting a cool breeze flow through. They entered the middle room, which was crowded with junk, had a TV on the wall, and had a round table in the middle. The back door was propped open, behind the table. It looked like a normal room.

They sat down.

Drake heard a buzzing noise. He waved his hand around his head, and it went away.

"So, what the heck just happened anyway?" Nellie asked. "The last thing we remember was the minute Drake touched that ball thing, we ended up spinning like crazy and hitting the ground."

Lorelei looked quite unexcited. Drake had had a slight wonder if she'd find it amazing like they did. "Well," the sorceress said, "you touched one of the portals. When you touch one, you get transported from one place to another, be it a few miles or a few dimensions." She paused. "Did you two come from earth?"

They nodded quickly.

She continued, "Long ago, soon after discovering earth, Uni's people set up portals all over your world. They wanted to learn about the lives you guys lived, and find some benefits. And we still do." She pointed to the television. "Well pretty soon people of Earth started finding the portals, and ending up in Uni. It wasn't good." She paused again.

Drake and Nellie leaned forward a little at the annoyingly cliffhanger-ish pauses.

"When they discovered them, they wanted to take the unicorns to earth. But they belong here. Unicorns need very pure air, as well as pure lifestyle. I fear they would die of sadness in another world full of pollution and stuff. So, of course, not wanting the unicorns to get hurt, the Uni people destroyed most of the portals, and since then hardly anyone from Earth ever finds this place. It's a whole different dimension." She said quietly.

"Wow." Drake said. "Maybe that's how the idea of unicorns came to Earth!"

"So, they're real. What are the unicorns like here?" asked Nellie, putting her elbows on the table and resting her chin in her hands. "I thought they were all white, had beards, and spoke telepathically or something like that."

Lorelei squinted her eyes. "Naw. They come in all colors, much like your horses. There are many different kinds, like the Arab unicorn. They all have different kinds of horns, and a lot of them have wings too. And like I said, they can learn to talk by listening to their owners and other humans."

"Arab unicorns?" Drake asked.

Lorelei nodded. "You'll hear a lot of familiar breeds, I think. Some of the Uni people went to your Arabia, and brought back some of the horses they found there. The horses bred to the unicorns and they came up with Arab unicorns. Many, many of the breeds here are influenced by yours."

Drake and Nellie's heads were spinning with information. Never had they dreamed of such a thing!

Drake was about to ask another question when he heard the buzzing sound again. Annoyed, he swiped at what he though was a bug. He heard a "SQUEEK" and a "PUHH" and a little creature that looked like a flying multicolored seahorse fell on the table, dazed.

"Noopie!" Lorelei fussed, picking up the little thing. It squeaked weakly in response.

"What did I hit?" asked Drake warily.

Lorelei was busy stroking the poor thing's tiny neck. "This is Noopie, my pet. He's a Qupdoodle." She said after it seemed to regain itself a bit.

"A qup-what?" Nellie said in confusion.

"He's very magical, and he helps me with my deeds."

"Deeds?"

"My deeds. My job. I help people with things. Anything. Hair color, sickness, you name it. That is what I do for a living."

"So you're a good sorceress?" Drake asked. "You won't nuke me while my back is turned or something like that?"

"No. That'd be Valerie."

Drake thought for a moment. Then he spotted a picture on the wall. It seemed to be of a racehorse. It was a gray, complete with jockey and saddle, and across its shoulders draped a blanket of roses. Of course, it had a horn on its forehead. Unicorn.

"What is that picture from?" Drake asked, pointing.

Something flashed across Lorelei's face for a moment. A tad of excitement? "That's a picture of Smoke Shadow. They call him the silver bullet."

"That's an awesome name," Nellie said.

"I think he was the greatest," Lorelei replied, nodding. "He won Uni's Triple Crown, and only lost twice his whole career."

That's kind of like Wisp, thought Drake.

"So Uni has horse – excuse me, unicorn races?" asked Nellie. "How old do you have to be to be a jockey?"

"Over 15, under around 5'7, and weight of no more than 115 pounds, if I may remember correctly."

"That means I could be a jockey," Drake said. He was only 5'4 and weighed a wimpy 111 pounds. He was almost 16.

"Well, so could I," Nellie said. "In six months, on my birthday."

Then, of course, Drake went into dreaming mode and sat there drooling.

"What kind of unicorns do you race?" Nellie asked while Drake was out of it.

"Oh, any kind of unicorn or horse is allowed to race. It's mostly thoroughbreds though. They kill off all of the competition. Though, there have been some pretty good non thoroughbreds too. Twilight, Quiet Sunrise…"

"You have regular horses here, too?

"Well, not exactly regular. They can still talk and are intelligent just like unicorns, except they don't have the horn, therefore cannot heal or stab anything. They still possess a bit of magic."

Lorelei got up and went into the kitchen. The room was so small that she didn't even need to shout, "Do you want anything to eat?"

Drake was too excited to eat. He was still trying to figure out what this was. Was it really the land of unicorns? Was he dreaming? He hated those darn stories where the character went on one of those huge adventures and then at the end they found out that it was only a dream. It would be so cool if it were real... he would never have to go to school or eat TV dinners again!

Nellie was thinking the same thing. She hoped there was no school in unicorn world. Nellie hated school.

Lorelei returned to the table, with a strange, purple drink. Drake stared at it. Was this some sort of strange magical sorceress drink?

"This is soda I turned purple," Lorelei said, noticing Drake's look and about reading his mind.

"I take it you like purple a lot," said Nellie.

"Yep. Noopie's lucky I don't turn *him* purple. And Alidar. And Valerie."

"Can we go outside and look around?" Drake asked.

"Sure. Just don't go far. The forest can be dangerous."

Drake stopped, suddenly feeling nervous. "What? Dangerous in what way?"

"It is the endless forest, after all. If you go at least three miles further, you end up in it. See, it's like the core of this forest around the outside of the house. There's a lot of deep magic in there. No creatures, because they know to stay away, but a lot of the trees have absorbed up the magic and become portals. It gets to a point where the invisible portals start up, then you never know where you'll end up, or if you'll be able to get back."

Drake hesitated, and was about to ask if she had ever gotten lost in there herself, but Nellie grabbed his arm and dragged him out, eager to explore, before he could. They stepped off of the house's small porch and down to the grass.

"Say, where was the place we fell?" she asked, looking around.

"I think it was right there," Drake answered, pointing to a stump. He went to one of the trees. It had hard gray bark. Pinecones littered the ground around it. It was hardly any different from the trees he knew!

The sound of fast hoof beats came to their ears, and they turned and saw Valerie and Alidar galloping back. Alidar was stretched out low, flying over the level ground, legs flying. But He wasn't running nearly as fast as a racehorse, Drake thought. No super unicorn speed for him.

Alidar came to a stop feet away from them, and Valerie jumped off.

When her feet hit the ground nimbly, she looked at Drake. "What are you doing staring at the tree?" she asked.

"I wasn't staring at the tree. I was examining it." Drake said.

Nellie had slipped over. She put a hand out and stroked Alidar's nose. Alidar raised his head, his eyes getting larger, nervously and sidestepped. "Could you…" he began to mumble.

"Calm down, Alidar. You're such a suspicious fellow!" Valerie boomed in a bright voice, poking him in the shoulder.

Just then, Drake looked off into the distance. On the long plains, he caught site of a pair of ears and eyes peeking over the same hill Valerie and Alidar had disappeared over earlier.

The ears became more, and then, a herd of unicorns of all colors galloped into sight and turned, then quickly disappeared into the forest to the left. Drake nearly jumped out of his skin, and barely noticed that some had horns, but most didn't.

"Did you see that glory of unicorns run by?" he said to Nellie and Valerie.

"That *herd* of unicorns, you mean," Valerie commented. "They're only called glories in *storybooks* you know."

That woman was beginning to annoy Drake.

"Come on, Nellie, let's follow them!" He said. Together, they started running towards the spot where the unicorns had gone.

"Wait!" Valerie yelled after them. "You'll never catch

them, they've probably disappeared already. Besides, they're wild... and, erm, they'll eat you!"

Drake sighed and turned back. Such a beautiful bay pinto mare had led the herd. If only he could own a horse like that.

"They will *NOT!*" Nellie said back to Valerie's last words.

Valerie giggled a little. "Just seeing what you knew." She looked at Drake, whom she seemed more interested in. "Ok, cheer up, if you want to ride a horse, you can ride Alidar here. He's smooth to ride, and only 14 hands high."

Alidar looked quite nervous about this. "You're going to just let this guy you've never met before ride me?" he squeaked. But Drake was already running towards him. He had never ridden a horse before, and now he would get the chance to ride a unicorn!

He skidded to a stop when he reached Alidar, who was staring back at him with a big green eye. Suddenly he looked so much larger. But Drake grabbed some of his mane and hoisted himself onto his broad back like he had seen done so much in movies.

Nothing happened. Alidar just stood there. His black-tipped ears were flicked back slightly.

"Well, gallop off into the sunset or something!" Drake

urged. Alidar broke into a fast trot, and Drake found himself bouncing all around, then down on the ground as Alidar snorted and came back around to look at him. He jumped back on in a flash, and Alidar once again trotted. But then he broke into a smooth canter and went in a big circle around them. Then, suddenly, he broke from the canter into a flying gallop, pounding out across the plains. Drake could barely hang on!

He couldn't think. He didn't realize how hard he was gripping, and he was hunched over, his form new and inexperienced. He held onto the wild black mane with both hands, knowing he'd be a grass pizza if he let go.

Alidar turned wide, as to not throw Drake off of balance too bad, and pointed back to the little gray house. He shot back towards it with a new intensity. It was an amazing speed, almost like he was moving so fast he was still beneath Drake. As the house rapidly approached, he began to slow, then, unexpectedly, stopped like a reining horse. Drake achieved his dream of flying and then hit a patch of grass.

"Are you okay?" Nellie said, running over. Before Drake answered, she decided he wasn't injured and said, "I want to ride him now!"

"Well I think there was a pine cone in there somwh…" Drake grumbled sorely as she left him.

She ran back and jumped onto Alidar's back, losing her balance for a moment, then she tightened her legs and clucked to him like she had seen in the movies. He took off across the plain again. Only this time when he stopped, he seemed gentler, and Nellie managed to stay on. Drake grumbled something about Alidar being easy on her because she was a girl and came over for another ride.

Poor Alidar was sweating and puffing, looking from Drake to Nellie and to Valerie, as if expecting a great reward.

"Hey, that's enough riding for him to last for a while," Valerie said, pulling a small piece of what looked like candy out of her pocket and letting Alidar have it.

Drake wasn't down a bit. He wanted to explore some more, but he didn't want to get lost on the plains or in the woods. He hoped Lorelei would show them around. Then a thought struck him. How would they get back to earth?

They patted Alidar thankfully before he told them that he preferred scratching so they scratched him thankfully instead. Nellie gave him a hug on the neck.

"Lorelei!" Drake soon called, turning away from the scene. "How do we get back to earth?" he called, stepping towards the house.

"You go back through the portal, simply." She called back

from inside. Then this was followed by a "D'oh!" and she came out of the open door again.

"Sorry Drake, I can't tell you where the portal back is because I can't trust you." She rubbed the back of her neck, for the first time, seeming irked.

"Why don't you trust me? I'd never hurt an animal," Drake replied. "And neither would Nellie. And I want to become a jockey! Here!"

Unfortunately, she didn't even appear thoughtful about it. "I still don't trust you yet. I'm sorry, to both of you."

Drake grumbled. So he could get back, but after he earned Lorelei's trust. Somehow, he didn't even want to leave. He wanted to jump on another unicorn's back and run all over Uni!

"Whaddya mean you don't trust us!?" Nellie asked loudly, going up to the open doorway and looking in with her hands on her hips.

"I mean I don't trust you, simple. Here, entertain yourself and don't harass me!" A book flew out from inside, and Nellie caught it with an *Oomph*. It was a big, worn out brown book that was as thick as a big dictionary. It didn't look too stimulating.

Nellie dusted off the cover. "Unicorn breeds of Uni!" she read. She trotted down the steps, set it down on the stump they had landed next to at first and opened it. Drake came over to look.

ARAB UNICORN

"Arab unicorns. It has all the information about them in here on this page!" Nellie said. She flipped to another page, one with a solid black horse with glowing red eyes, fangs, and a mane that flowed like pure midnight.

"That's a scary looking one. It says it's a Nightmare. They are always black with red eyes and their manes and tails are made of darkness."

"How is that possible?" Drake asked.

"I don't know, but I sure wouldn't want to meet up with one of them in a dark alley, that's for sure. They eat meat, including other horses."

"I met one of them once," Alidar said, coming over. "They're nuts, and that's what makes them able to eat another horse. Luckily, they can't run that fast and they only come out at night."

"That's good." Nellie flipped to another page. "Palomino ponies! Oh look how cute and happy they are!"

"The little wimps of Uni," Alidar scoffed. "They're only for little kids and mediocre riders. Everyone thinks they're so cute…"

"I sure do. It says they're always palomino with four white socks and a blaze. They make very good children's mounts and would never hurt a fly."

"Okay, turn the page already!" Alidar said, clearly uninterested in the ponies. (Probably because he sort of looked like one build-wise.)

The next page was one of a white unicorn. It was pearly, long, and lean, with a long mane and tail that were so smooth they seemed to be made from cloud. Or whipped cream. Or something pleasant like that.

"I like that one," Drake said admiringly. "What's it say about it?" He looked at the page. It said:

Cloud Unicorns

Sometimes called Rain Appaloosas

Height: 14 to 17 hands

Temperament: usually calm and cool

Color: always white, with sun-proof white skin

Horn type: A

Wing type: A

Cloud unicorns live high in the clouds of Uni's lands. They are usually quite friendly, and very intelligent. They live in medium sized herds on strange, solid clouds that are very unlike regular clouds, though they look nearly the same. Their diet is composed of cloud berries (see index pg. IV) and water from rain pools. They are known for their silky smooth manes and tails, and their strange, not pink or black, but white skin that can't seem to be harmed by the sun's rays. The reason some people call them Rain Appaloosas is because when it rains, every raindrop that hits their hide makes a spot of a different color of the rainbow. They go away after they dry off.

"Wow," said Drake. "I wish I had one of those."

"They have weak soft hooves," grumbled Alidar.

"I want to go and explore some more now," Nellie said.

She got up and started walking deeper into the trees on her own accord. Drake left the book lying open and ran after. Alidar followed worriedly.

There was a worn out path through this part of the forest. The grass was so soft and springy, and there were small white and yellow flowers sprouting out of the ground. There was slight sunshine and sunrays coming down and lighting the grass.

Looks like something out of a Disney movie, Drake thought.

Nellie suddenly stopped short, causing Drake to run into her. Following just as closely, Alidar nearly sat down, trying not to run over them.

"Hey! What gives, Nellie?"

"Stream."

Then, he saw that there was a small stream in the way. Nellie bent down and looked into the water. It was about a foot deep. The bottom was made of beautiful rounded stones and pebbles. She reached down blindly and picked one up.

All three gazed at it. It was glassy smooth and pinkish white, un-opaque and shiny. It was filled with cracks on the inside, much like quartz, but it did not break. Nellie turned and put it in Drake's pocket.

"Hey!" said Drake again. "What am I, your pack mule?"

"Well, I don't have any pockets, so yours will do. I think. If they don't have lord knows what in them." She rolled her eyes, and bent down again.

Alidar watched, his ears pricked.

She got two more of the pretty stones, a yellowish one and a sparkly black one. Then she reached down to pick up another, and she felt something slimy between her fingers.

"OH!" she said, holding a red fish by the tail. It flopped back into the water. She shook her hand.

"You disturbed its nest," Alidar said quietly. Then, the two humans watched in amazement as the fish picked up another stone in its mouth, and dropped it where the one Nellie took had been. It was very picky, zigzagging through the water and then finding the perfect one.

"It's being careful not to disturb another's fish's home," Alidar commented. "We shouldn't walk through this stream."

They continued on parallel to the stream until they came to a huge tree. It had hundreds of branches on it; it was so big and tall.

Of course, Nellie wanted to climb it!

"You are so immature," Drake scoffed, as she stepped on

a low branch and began to climb her way up. They lost sight of her soon.

She climbed quickly. Soon, the branches Nellie was grabbing were starting to feel like ropes, bending under her weight. Then she looked to see how high she was. She was almost above the tops of the gray trees. Her heart lurched. She hadn't known she was this high!

She held fast to the branches and now stayed still, looking around some more. She felt she could see forever, or at least until the trees ended. Then there was just green. So far away, to the side, there was an ocean. At least she thought it was an ocean, unless it was a mirage. There were visible specks across the green in one place. A herd of unicorns?

The sun was high in the sky. Nellie guessed it was about 2 o' clock in the afternoon. Did Uni have the same time as earth? She looked up. There were a few fluffy white clouds. Were those cloud unicorn's clouds? Suddenly, a brown dot flew over her. She looked up. It was a flying horse – no, a unicorn – or a pegacorn? – feathery wings outstretched. She whistled to it.

It quickly turned its head and saw her. Then it went flying away real quickly, towards the specks on the grass far away. It must've been wild.

Soon she heard Drake and Alidar calling from the forest

floor, which now seemed like a really boring place compared to this. She wanted to fly high in the sky up there, on a magnificent raven black unicorn. He would only let her ride him, and he would be the fastest in the land...

She started stepping back down the tree. It took a while... suddenly she heard a snap, and the limb under her foot broke! Then she was falling fast, towards the treetops of the gray trees that were so surprisingly tall. The falling sensation was real this time.

Beside Drake, there was a sudden flap of wide wings, almost like an umbrella being opened quickly. With the wind still blowing his hair sideways, he caught blurred glimpses of Alidar jumping into the air and flying towards Nellie. She managed to catch his mane and fly down with him, then flop into the grass harmlessly.

Drake nudged her with his foot teasingly. Alidar looked nervous again, folding the feathered black wings that had suddenly seemed to appear to his sides.

"Let's go back now," he said, shaking his mane.

"I didn't know you could fly," Drake replied. At this point, he was open to anything. "How do you just make your wings appear like that?"

Alidar wasn't a unicorn into explaining. "Magicalness." He said simply.

With that, he folded them back into his sides in a burst of sparkles. They seemed to disappear. His back was bare again.

Drake and Nellie gawked and gawked and gawked.

Chapter 3

Drake Attempts to Find Free Real Estate

The three walked back to Lorelei's house. Lorelei was now out-side, and standing in the front yard with a dragon as Noopie buzzed around her head. Drake and Nellie stopped short, but Alidar kept walking like it was nothing. Valerie was sitting on the house's small front porch, eating a sandwich.

Drake stared. The dragon was orange, with a yellow bel-ly. It was standing on its two hind legs. It had a fairly long neck, and the top of its head had three spikes on it, almost like a spiky hairdo. It saw Drake and Nellie staring at it and smiled and waved for a moment. Drake gawked. That was NOT the kind of response he was expecting.

The dragon and Lorelei seemed to be in the middle of something. She motioned for it to wait outside while she went into the house. Drake and Nellie eyed it warily and went inside after her.

"Lorelei! What's that dragon doing there?" Nellie asked, clearly about to have a heart attack.

Lorelei replied, "That's Zenny. He comes around sometimes. He has small wings and can't fly, but there's not a way I know of to grow dragon wings quickly, so I just give him soda dyed purple and tell him its potion."

"Won't he get angry and burn you to death or something if he finds out?"

"He can't breathe fire either. I would call him a defective dragon. Don't worry, he's a very nice guy."

Drake felt a little better. "What time is it?"

"Two hours past lunchtime. 2 o' clock."

"What are we going to do when we have to go back home?"

"You won't go back home."

Darn it, thought Drake. "Then can I live here?"

"Around here if you want. But don't think I'm sharing my house with any more people."

46

"Ok. I'm going to catch a Unicorn and become a jockey and race it!"

"Well, good luck trying to catch one. They won't appreciate that very much."

"We'll see about that. They can't resist me. And I officially claim... that spot over there!" Drake said, pointing to a clearing of trees.

"There? Only if you can convince Sunridge to share," Lorelei said, smiling.

"Eh?"

Nellie stood next to them with her hands behind her back.

"There's a herd of unicorns led by Sunridge, a stallion, that goes over there and sleeps every night. Alidar came from that herd."

"Okay...then can I go back to my home?" he tried again. If he could just know he could go back and forth, maybe bring his family...

"No!"

"Then can I live in your house?"

"NO!"

"Then can I go hom..."

"No! If you leave I'll destroy the portal so you won't be able to get back!"

"But my mom will be worried!"

Nellie turned to Drake. "Do you really think mom wants two more kids that she can hardly even feed? Maybe it *would* be better if we stayed here."

"Yeah…but we can't just let her think we died or something."

"You can send her a letter." Lorelei offered.

"Hellooo… we're in like separate worlds!" Drake said, this time being the smarty one.

"And I have a wand and Alidar."

Alidar, who was listening from beside the porch, turned and ran.

"You can write a letter saying where you are, and then I'll turn Alidar into a bird, and he can fly the letter to your house."

Alidar ran even faster.

"I guess that sounds all right," Drake said.

Valerie walked in, burped, and said that Zenny was wondering what was taking so long. Lorelei poured a soda into a glass, pointed her wand at it, chanted something, and the drink turned purple.

"Do you have to cheat Zenny like that?" Nellie asked.

"It isn't like I make him pay," said Lorelei. "And like I

said, there's no way I know to make his wings any bigger. They have to grow on their own."

She walked back outside. Drake and Nellie followed. Zenny was sitting on the stump with Alidar hanging out close by, sort of hidden behind him. When Zenny saw them, he turned towards them, and his tail accidentally whacked Alidar's little legs out from beneath him. And with all the luck, knocked him out.

"Oh my... gobble! Alidar!" Lorelei said, running over to Alidar who was lying unconscious on the ground.

"Oh no! I'm sorry!" Screeched Zenny, horrified. His voice was high and nervous. "I didn't mean to do that!! I swear!!"

Lorelei poured the purple 'potion' soda all over Alidar and he woke up with a snort.

"@%#^ it, Lorelei I could have woken up on my own!" he said.

Everyone gasped. "Alidar!"

"What? So I said what I was thinking. And *you,*" he said pointing at Zenny, "Are a bumbling, tail-wagging insult to dragons!"

Zenny looked guilty. "I said I was sorry, and Lorelei used my potion to wake you up... I guess you could have had it anyway..." his wings drooped.

Alidar humphed and turned and went around to the other side of the house.

"Sorry I threw the potion all over him, but it probably wouldn't have worked anyways, so..." Lorelei said.

Zenny trudged away sadly.

"Well that was easy."

"Lorelei! That's evil!" Nellie said. "Don't you care about his feelings? And that Alidar needs a good... er, well, he needs it good!"

Lorelei laughed, surprising them. "Oh, Valerie is probably telling him off for cussing right now," Lorelei said. "He listens to her better than me."

Drake was still surprised at how Zenny had been. "Are all of the dragons here like that?" He asked.

"No. Zenny is just a wimp. Usually the dragons around here are friendly and docile. Most of them are herbivorous, too. Zenny is just an extra, extra docile one. He eats salads, for goodness sakes!

Nellie snorted.

"All right. So if we're going to live here," Drake said, "we should go and make a place to sleep now.

"Have fun," said Nellie.

"Oh no! You're helping!"

Drake made Nellie go off into the woods and find sticks,

while he picked up pinecones off the ground of his selected space. Valerie rode Alidar over and watched.

"Don't you ever use a saddle?" Drake asked her.

"No. Would you want a big hunk of leather strapped onto your back, squeezing you to death?"

"I think I would fall off a lot if I didn't wear a saddle, judging from how I rode Alidar this morning."

"Well, Alidar does have small withers." Valerie slid off and landed on her feet.

Nellie walked up behind Alidar just then, holding a bundle of sticks. She quietly pulled one out of the bundle, waited until Alidar's attention was on something else, and poked him with it firmly. He squealed and jumped about four feet in the air, and whirled around to face the attacker. Nellie was snickering.

For a moment Alidar looked like he was going to say every cuss word known to unicorns, but then thought better and turned and trotted off. Nellie was still snickering.

"Nellie! That's no way to be to a unicorn! He'll probably nuke you when your back is turned or something!" Drake said.

He took the bundle of sticks and attempted to make something with them. He failed.

Valerie laughed and followed after Alidar.

"Forget these kinds of sticks. We need two long ones that are bendable." Drake said, ignoring her.

Nellie grumbled off and Drake started to tear a long piece of gray bark off of a tree. Lorelei called from inside, seeming to know–

"DON'T HARM THE TREES!!"

Guiltily Drake put the bark back and patted it innocently. He found some big leaves on the ground to use instead.

Drake was ready now. Nellie was taking a long time. Finally, she came running back with two long sticks. "You won't believe what I saw!"

"Maybe I will. After all, I do think I am nuts and hallucinating for where we are now."

"Well, there I was innocently picking up these sticks when I heard something crashing through the woods behind me. So I turned around, and there was this unicorn standing there! Actually it didn't have a horn, but it was fiery red and its mane and tail *were* fire! I know they were! I thought it was going to burn the forest and me down, but it snorted at me and just walked off like it was nothing. Seriously, it was a horse on fire!"

Drake looked at her strangely. "Maybe it will say something about it in that unicorn book Lorelei gave us."

They both went over to where the book was still lying

on the ground. Drake had no clue what to do so he looked up "Fire" in the index. "Fire mane" showed up. He turned to the page.

"That's what I saw," Nellie said, pointing to a picture of a red horse with a flaming crest and tail.

"Now I've seen everything," Drake said.

"It says they live in underground caverns under fiery mountains in Unicorabia. All right, now what's with that? We are NOT in Arabia, or Unicorabia, or whatever it is. I think."

"It must have been owned by someone who was letting it run around free." Valerie said. She was standing right behind Drake again. Drake jumped a foot in the air.

"Why would somebody want to own a horse that would catch them on fire if they tried to pet it?"

"Silly, they don't catch them on fire." She just tossed her mane and turned away.

Drake remembered what they were doing and took the two sticks and stuck them into the ground. Then he bent them and stuck them in the ground again, so they were like two little arches side by side. Then he attempted to use vines and tie sticks on the top but they kept falling off. Drake said a bad word loudly.

Valerie took pity on him and brought him some sticky

tape. Drake taped big leaves to the top of the arches. Now he had a little shelter about two feet wide.

"That's not big enough for the both of us," said Nellie, unimpressed.

That night they both were lying on the ground under their shelter (which Drake had made another addition to so it was more like four feet wide) and were staring at the moon that was rising off in the distance. They could see it through the trees. The sky was, of course, beautiful and full of orange and purple and pink and the stars shone much more brightly than the ones the siblings knew. And the moon was huge. Beside it there was another moon, like a light shadow, a quarter the size or it. So there were two moons, or a moon with a smaller moon, or whatever you call it – but it was awesome.

Then they noticed dark figures coming towards them through the trees. Nellie squeaked.

"Shh." Drake shushed. "The herd."

The mare in the lead was the pretty bay pinto, straight-faced, wide-nosed and intelligent looking. Beside her was a much bigger, thicker horse that must have been the stallion. He was a strange color, with the golden and black body of a dun or buckskin, but a white mane and tail. He looked stocky and strong, and his features immediately made Drake think of Alidar. A thick, ivory horn adorned his broad forehead. He snorted and walked forward, his eyes never leaving Nellie and Drake. They weren't very well hidden.

The herd fanned out among the trees, some looking curiously over. The buckskin/palomino kept them away from the humans, but he did not seem to care that they were there, and began to doze when they were settled.

Drake and Nellie were content to watch the pretty animals shining in the moonlight, until they fell asleep.

By the time they woke up the next morning, the herd was long gone. It was still a bit early, and a cool breeze blew through the trees. It felt like spring. If Drake had been back on earth he would have been waiting anxiously for summer break.

They got up and stretched and walked around for an hour, not sure what to do. Lorelei and Valerie had not come out of their house yet. Drake stepped in stallion poo, which was worse than the average poo, he learned.

They had gotten their clothes pretty dirty, and now they both realized they had nothing else to wear. They went and sheepishly knocked on Lorelei's door.

She and her sister were awake and sitting at their table. Alidar was looking in the window from the other side of the house and looked disturbingly like a black forelocked and plain-faced Mr. Ed.

Lorelei pitied them. "I don't know what to do with you," she said. "You can't go back to your world but there's not enough room in my house for you."

"If you give us food, we can sleep in that shelter we made until we work something out," Nellie suggested hungrily. She just realized she hadn't eaten dinner before. Or lunch!

"Well, maybe," said Lorelei. "But you need to get a job or something so you can have your own money."

"What?" Drake said. From what he had seen, Uni was all trees and endless grasslands.

"There is a city not too far away from here where you could find something," Lorelei said. However, how you would get there, I do not know."

"Couldn't you just teleport us there or something?"

"No, I dunno how to teleport yet."

"What about Alidar?"

"I'm not sure I trust you guys together..." she raised an eyebrow playfully. "Not now."

"Oh well... guess I'd better find my own unicorn, then," Drake said, suddenly very hopeful. Once again, his mind filled with thoughts. If he caught a unicorn for himself! He would have a horse! A TALKING horse! One that would not buck or rear or anything that some regular horses did!

Nellie also was dreaming of her black horse, one who would only allow her to ride it and be the fastest horse in the land...

"Unicorns *are* hard to catch," Lorelei warned. "It is much better to befriend them. And talk to them, because they learn human speech almost automatically on hearing words, and one may talk back to you if you say enough. Alidar listens to us and knows many, many words now."

Drake and Nellie were excited. They wanted to go exploring, and see all the unicorns, then try to befriend them, and then most fun of all (for Drake), RACE them!

Lorelei poked Drake in the stomach. He came back down to earth and went "oof." Then before he forgot he said "Do you have any clothes we could borrow, please?"

So Drake and Nellie ended up going and exploring the forest again out of boredom, because there was no herd of horses anywhere around for miles, it seemed. Nellie was not in as much a hurry as Drake, because she wanted to take her time and find the *perfect* horse. It wouldn't hurt for it to be even faster than Drake's, she thought evilly.

Nellie, now wearing pink colored denim pants and a black tank top exclaimed when she saw the place she had seen the fire horse. "Look, that's where I saw that weird horse!"

"Whoa! Dude! The leaves are all singed!" said Drake, wearing regular blue denim jeans and a white shirt.

They followed the burnt leaves until the trees started to thin, and they could see more grasslands beyond. Nellie stepped out of a bush and tripped over a stake.

"Hey look, it's a tent," Drake said, paying her no mind.

Nellie cursed him madly for not helping her up.

Drake went around to the front of the triangle-shaped tent. It was green and blended in with the scenery. And it was big. Big enough for a horse, even. But there was no horse in it, or person, anywhere around.

"I wonder who it belongs to," wondered Nellie aloud. But Drake looked farther on, on the grass.

"There!" he said.

The fire horse was there, all right, with its reddish brown coat gleaming. It had a saddle on, and Drake recognized it as a type of racing saddle. On the saddle was a girl with long wavy hair almost as red as the horse. She was wearing blue jeans like Drake's, and a red T shirt that fit almost as tightly as the jeans. She actually looked more like she was trying to attract boys than ride her horse.

Drake thought she looked hot. Really. She didn't seem to be catching on fire, though. Her horse wasn't burning her.

She drew her reins up and they went into a canter, and cantered around some. Drake and Nellie started walking over there. The horse noticed them out of the corner of its eye, and nickered to its rider.

They noticed the trio, and cantered over.

"Hi" said Drake.

"Hello there. Do you want an autograph or something?" she asked right off, tilting her head almost cockily. Not *quite* that far, yet.

"What for?" Nellie asked, a little annoyed with the greeting.

"From the fastest horse in Uni, of course," she said, sure of herself. "The one who runs like a quarter horse. For more than just a quarter."

The fiery horse snorted, as if agreeing.

"You race it?" asked Drake.

"Of course I race HER, and we've won so many races it'll make your head blow off!" She grinned a huge grin.

"I don't want my head to blow off," said Drake nervously.

"I'm just saying that because I need something cooler than 'Make your head spin'," the redhead said. "And my horse has never lost, so, yeah."

Nellie was annoyed by her. When she got her black horse she would have to remember to kick her butt in a race.

"Want to see her gallop?" The redhead asked slyly, playing with her reins.

"Sure," said Drake, going along with everything she said.

In an instant, the girl and the horse turned, cantered off (sending dirt clods Drake and Nellie's way, making Nellie very frustrated and Drake even more in awe) then disappeared on the other side of a hill. Drake soon heard rapid hoof beats, and they came flying back, the redhead crouching expertly over her horse's withers and neck. She allowed a pretty loose rein. Legs and fire streaming tail a long blur, they flew past, slowed, then turned around and galloped in the other direction. Her horse seemed not to touch the ground as she galloped, her legs went too fast, but Drake knew she wasn't flying because of her thundering hoof beats. Drake gulped and wondered how long that horse could run like that. That was definitely as fast as his dream horse, and maybe faster. Now he needed a really, really fast horse to beat that one.

The horse stopped and puffed, and trotted back to Nellie and Drake.

"She is fast," said Nellie, amazed. "She does run like a quarter horse."

"How is it that you aren't getting burned?" asked Drake, for now the horse's fire seemed to blaze even stronger.

"Songoffire can control her own fire," said the girl, looking offended. "Don't you know about fire horses?"

Is that her horse's name? Nellie thought. Her horse would have a cool name, like Nighthawk or some awesome thing like that.

Before Drake could admit that he didn't know *anything* about fire horses, the redhead spoke again, clearly bored. "Well, we have to go on our daily long walk now," she said, turning Songoffire. "We'll see you later." And they trotted off.

Gosh, she's hot, thought Drake.

@$#%!!, thought Nellie.

They went back into the forest after she disappeared from sight. Drake was starting to think he'd have to look really hard to find a wild horse or unicorn that was that fast.

And Nellie knew what he was thinking. "Drake, she warned, "you don't need a horse *that* fast to win. That horse took such small strides, I doubt it would have lasted in any race over six furlongs."

"Yeah, but I wonder if there are any wild horses that fast... that horse was probably bought by that girl, shipped from Uni-a-rabia or whatever it was called."

"Drake, you need to think about why you want a horse. Back home you would take a donkey. Now you want to buy a fancy unicorn. I thought all you wanted was a friend in your horse," she said.

"Yeah," Drake said glumly. He looked up at the sky, as if to see cloud unicorns flying around up there.

They came back to Lorelei's house at noon. They were disappointed that they hadn't seen any cool Uni animals. They saw some cool birds though... as far as birds can go being cool.

Drake asked Alidar if he would let him ride him so they could go looking for wild horses/unicorns.

"Why do you want a wild horse-slash-unicorn so much? They're full of inbreeding and poor conformation!" he whined.

"Quit being lazy and take him, Alidar." Lorelei made him. So Drake rode him without a saddle or bridle, with a death grip on his mane. Nellie had not really wanted to come. She told him that if he saw any good looking black horses tell her. She would rather not ride around double with sweaty ol' Drake.

"Why are you always so reluctant?" asked Drake, tired of silence while riding Alidar.

Alidar was reluctant to answer (duh). "I... I don't like doing stuff... the other horses don't like me."

Drake petted him calmingly. He definitely wanted a braver horse, but he was fine for the time being. He liked riding.

They came near one herd, which was spread out grazing in the tall grass. The stallion was a pretty grey color, with an enormous roman nose and short little legs. Drake saw one horse (there was only a couple of real unicorns in this herd) he liked, a colorful palomino pinto colt, but it too had a roman nose and a big belly, and it didn't seem to be alert that the unfamiliar human and unicorn were even passing. And it was only a young one. There were no black horses in the herd, either.

They decided to keep looking. They went far. Drake saw the redheaded girl once again, far off in the distance, cantering, but she did not see him. And they went past two dragons, spiky headed ones like Zenny, who were dozing good naturedly. Drake squeezed Alidar tensely, and he popped a small buck in annoyance. "Chill!"

The next herd they saw was better, but no luck. Drake saw a little black mare, but she looked older and was in foal.

Her yearling was dark grey and Drake though he was pretty but too young. He wanted a horse he could ride right away!

"Alidar, can we fly?" asked Drake, remembering. So, in a swirl of Magicalness, Alidar flapped his wings out, making Drake fly... off. Alidar snickered as he got back on.

Drake sat on Alidar's withers (Thanking goodness they *were* small and mutton-y) and Alidar flew slowly up in the air. They glided around, going higher and higher, until Drake got freaked out and wanted to go lower. The clouds were close now. He looked up at one. Was it his imagination or was there a cloud unicorn looking down?

They glided down. Suddenly Drake heard faint hoof beats and looked beneath them. There was a white horse galloping slowly under them, chasing their shadow. Drake could not see it well, but it had a horn and a long mane and tail. Funny he should be looking to the clouds for a white horse, when one came up underneath!

It whinnied shrilly, playfully, and galloped past them, its tail raised up with excitement and nervousness of the things above its head that had taken notice of its run.

"Go down," Drake said, amused by the horse's playfulness. Alidar glided down until he was cantering on the ground. He stopped and looked at the white horse, which was standing on the top of a hill not far ahead.

Drake immediately liked this horse – or, Unicorn. She reared playfully, her eyes wide, pawing the air as if they were some sort of terrible monster she wished she hadn't been seen by. And yet, she didn't leave.

Drake glanced around. There were no other horses or unicorns nearby. The filly was alone. She let out a soft, curious whinny, and watched them, not still. She was very lean, not yet filled out completely. Her legs were long and gangly. She looked young. Drake was used to seeing young, lanky thoroughbreds at the track back home, and he would have guessed she'd be about three this spring. She would be a tall unicorn when fully grown, thought Drake.

She suddenly bolted off galloping, her tail high once more. It took a moment for her to get her long legs under control, and she sped past, pearly white shining with her silky mane and tail.

"Hey, wait!!" said Drake.

"She's showing off," said Alidar, his eyes following her.

They watched as she galloped off until she disappeared. Drake was disappointed she had not stayed. "Let's go after her," he said, but Alidar stayed still.

"We can do that tomorrow." He said. "We don't want to seem too interested."

It was getting late, so they cantered, with Drake's balance better, back to Lorelei's house. Drake told Nellie all about the filly and how he wanted to make friends with her.

"I'm sure she was a cloud unicorn," he said. "I think she had white skin. And she looked like she was going to be fast."

"Cool." Nellie seemed to regret not coming. "I want to come with you to see her next time!"

Alidar groaned.

Chapter 4

The Cloud Filly

The next day, sure enough, Alidar carried Nellie and Drake
all the way back to where they had seen the filly. Alidar was
tired from carrying two people, so they got off and walked for
a while. They searched around, but the filly was no where to
be seen. The only thing Drake saw as a reminder were a few
wide-spread galloping hoof prints in a line. He was sure they
were the filly's.

Drake had brought two carrots he got from Lorelei, just
in case, and he reached in his pocket and broke off a piece.

Alidar lipped it out of his hand happily, glad he was being paid somehow.

They passed the same herds along the way, but Nellie and Drake saw no horses they fancied. Drake's mind was completely on the filly. She was so different than the short, round bellied wild unicorns.

Then Drake saw a flash of light out of the corner of his eye, and far off in the distance, sure enough, was the filly. Her long, platinum colored horn reflected the sunlight, and the breeze rippled her silvery white mane and tail, not a touch of yellow in them.

"There she is," he said.

They admired her for a moment. Seeming to know, the filly turned and began to gallop away.

They scrambled back onto Alidar's back, and they took off galloping, almost making Nellie fly off the back. Galloping double bareback was NOT pleasant, thought Drake for a moment. Alidar ran gamely after the filly and for a bit he was catching her. She looked back over her shoulder and around her flagged tail and saw him, but she continued to spring along on her long legs as if she hadn't a care. She knew she could leave him behind easily. She let him catch up to her, but not come within 40 feet of her.

Alidar was puffing, but he had stamina. But carrying

an extra two hundred and something pounds on his 14 hand body made him slow, and the filly taunted him by slowing until he was within 15 feet of her, and then sped up, adding a few playful bucks.

Suddenly Alidar slipped on a rock and stumbled hard. He rocked his weight back onto his hindquarters, breaking down into a hobbling sort of gait. He stopped painfully. Drake and Nellie jumped off of him. He held his right front leg up and grunted with pain.

"My leg! I think it's broken," he said dramatically.

Nellie gently felt it, and he grunted again when she touched his knee. It was already starting to swell up.

"Your leg isn't broken, but you hurt your knee," Nellie said. "What happened?"

"I slipped on a rock, and that's why I stumbled, and I hit my knee," he said, examining his own leg. He winced and tried to walk, but his head flew down when he put weight on his bad leg.

Little tears of pain stained his coat, and Nellie stroked his neck softly. "I wonder what happened to the filly," she said.

"She's still there, look." Drake pointed to the horizon. The filly was watching them. She hesitantly took a step forward, and then tossed her head up and down. Another soft whinny came.

Alidar did not bother to answer her. He felt sorry for himself. *Besides*, the little buckskin thought, *she's an air headed show off!*

"You're a unicorn, can you heal yourself?" Nellie asked Alidar.

He shook his head. "Not myself." He said unhappily.

Drake felt bad and gave him some more of his carrot. "How are we going to get back?" he asked.

"I'll have to fly," replied Alidar.

"We can follow you on the ground," said Nellie. "You can't fly with us both weighing you down."

"OK, I will fly slowly," promised Alidar.

Going back was slow and hard. Nellie and Drake were not exactly champion long distance runners. They had to stop every few minutes, and Alidar flew around them while waiting.

Drake had noticed that the white filly was following them. They had not finished their chase. She probably wondered if Alidar was okay. She saw Drake looking back at her once, and turned around and trotted away. But when they started again, she still followed off in the distance.

She isn't even tired, Drake thought. *Where could her herd be?*

It was getting late, and the sun was lower in the sky when they returned. Valerie worried and fussed all over Alidar, who soaked up all the attention like a sponge. Drake and Nellie felt that it was their fault he had gotten hurt, and apologized to him, even though he unenthusiastically said that it wasn't their fault.

The filly had disappeared some time before. Drake guessed that she knew that a herd lived nearby. Any stallion, including Sunridge, the one who had the herd, would want her for his band of mares if he saw her.

They followed Valerie inside as she got her magic wand and came back out to Alidar. Alidar looked nervous.

"I think I can fix you," she said confidently.

Alidar did not like the way she said it, FIX you. "No, Valerie, I am quite fine!" he said nervously, tucking his tail (or trying to) and limping away.

When Lorelei came home (she had been in the forest gathering sorceress-y things like magical ingredients and plants and stuff) she examined Alidar's leg, and said that she did not know how to heal him because she didn't know what was wrong with it. It wasn't broken, but it didn't look sprained or twisted, either.

"That's the problem with healing spells," she said sheepishly. "You have to know exactly what's wrong to fix something."

Alidar had a stall behind their house, and Lorelei made it magically filled with twice the usual amount of wood shavings for Alidar to lie on. And he did lie there, for the rest of the day, with a pillow and a blanket and his little stuffed horse.

Drake gave him the last of his carrots and patted him, and Nellie felt bad for him and hugged him. Then they left the stall to go and wait for the wild herd to come in, for the sun was setting.

Soon the herd began to appear around the trees. Xochitl, the stallion, came first, and took his usual spot near them. Nellie had named him Xochitl because she came up with all the funkiest names that Drake couldn't pronounce. Drake had wanted to call him Buck.

The stallion looked at them, then yawned and flexed his muscles. His long white mane was thick and hot looking, and matted. It was making Nellie crazy.

She pulled out her trusty folding hairbrush/mirror (she always kept it in her pocket) and wriggled out from under the shelter. "You're going to brush his hair?" she heard Drake say. She ignored him and walked towards Xochitl. She hoped he was not afraid of people and could talk, because she also really wanted to ask him some stuff.

"Hi," she said, stopping a few feet away from him.

His eyes got wide and he looked at her, startled. "Hello," he responded nervously.

"You can talk," she said happily. "I'm Nellie."

"I'm Sunridge."

Nellie was glad he could speak her language. "My brother and I, we now live here."

"Uhhh... I noticed."

Softly she touched his shoulder. He didn't flinch. "Can I brush your mane?"

"Uhhh... sure."

Nellie started brushing madly, starting at the bottom. Sunridge/Xochitl almost lost his balance.

"So, have you seen any pretty black horses running around lately?"

"Why?"

"I like black horses," Nellie said. "Fun, fast black horses."

"I have seen no black horses," he said. "None that you would like."

"No fast ones?"

"Well, one is pretty fast, but he's kind of disturbed in the mind, and you just wouldn't like him."

"What exactly does he look like?"

Sunridge seemed to get into it. He looked down at his hooves. "He's solid black. No socks or anything. Longish black hair on the back of his fetlocks. And he has bluish purple eyes, I think. Horn of ebony. But it doesn't matter, because no one's seen him in a while. He must have jumped off a cliff or something."

"Oh." Nellie thought he sounded pretty. "Why's he disturbed?"

"He hates other horses and unicorns. He's always alone. I met him one time. Full brother to that Cloud Filly, they say. Word has it, he's of the same breed, but he fell from the clouds before he could fly, hit his head, and that's why he's nuts. Really, you'd not like him."

"Okay," Nellie said, interested. "Who's the Cloud Filly?"

"Do you know of that gangly white cloud unicorn filly that runs around on the ground? Also quite insane in the membrane. She has no herd, because no stallion can catch her. Believe me, I've tried."

"My brother tried to make friends with her today. She is curious," Nellie said. "We were following her and our unicorn got hurt so we had to stop."

"Alidar?"

"Yes. He tripped on a rock."

"He never was very sure footed."

Nellie finished combing his mane. "Well, I guess I'll go sleep now," she said. "By the way, how do you know how to talk?"

"I listen to the sisters in that house over there," he said.

"And I have to warn your brother, that filly will be hard to get... very hard in deed."

Nellie waved to him, causing him to blink in surprise, then went back and lay down again. "That stallion's name is Sunridge," was the only thing she told Drake. She was thinking about the black horse. She wished she could have met him. And a brother to the Cloud Filly? He would be fast... if he were alive. And pure black was the thing, with no socks or anything... how beautiful it would be.

Meanwhile, Sunridge tossed his smooth mane. He liked the new, brushed out smoothness. He tossed it again. He tossed his mane for a while as he thought about that Cloud filly. She was so pretty, he would have loved to have her in his herd – but she was so strange! She was much faster than him, a free roaming loner. Nellie's brother would never be able to catch her. Maybe he could befriend her if he was very patient, though. And if he really made her curious enough.

He thought of the black colt that never showed himself. He seemed to hate everyone around him. He would get into fights and then disappear. Sunridge figured he must have had some bad experience with other horses or something. He had gone up to him one day, unseen, and gently asked him what was wrong. The young unicorn looked upset, but only glared at him and trotted away into the shadows.

He really wouldn't have been surprised if the colt had been killed by an angry stallion, or died somehow, though it was saddening to think about.

Meanwhile, a certain white filly was silently making her way across the plains. Her build shone pearly and silky in the moonlight. She gazed at the sky as she walked. The moonlight reflected off the clouds, too. That was where her mother lived, and her little brother. Her cousins and grandparents, they all lived in the clouds in the magnificent herd of cloud unicorns.

The clouds did not suit her. She got tired of eating cloud berries (the berries that cloud unicorns live off of up there instead of grass) and bouncing around all the time. She just wanted to run, fast. No one could outrun her, not even her black brother Nightcloud, because before he had tried to catch her, but he lost her every time. That was back when they were younger, two year olds. She hadn't seen him for almost a year.

The filly's name given to her by her mother was Cloudberry. She was glad that it wasn't Skydancer or some name that everyone else had.

She was heading to where she had seen the humans and the unicorn go. She was very curious about the boy. He'd said hi to her! She had only seen four other humans before – the show-offy redheaded girl and her cocky fire horse, the purple-haired girl, the blonde girl, and a much darker redheaded guy who had a blue dragon. She didn't like the guy very much. She stayed away from his territories.

But this boy she saw seemed to be nice, and was nice to his buckskin unicorn, and rode it bareback, which, if she ever was ridden, was the way she wanted to be ridden. And he had a mate with him (Nellie!). She had been having fun running from them, but the next thing she knew when she looked back they were on the ground and their unicorn was hurt. She felt bad for him and wanted to try to heal him and see if she could learn more about the boy.

She came to the path that led into the woods and to the house. She was hesitant when she saw Sunridge's herd, but she knew that she could outrun him if he tried to capture her into his herd.

No lights were on in the house. She floated by, silent as moonlight, and smelled the air. She smelled the buckskin's scent. Yes, she had a very good nose. She had smelled the buckskin's scent as she had followed him earlier on, and re-membered it well.

She was curious about the stall behind the house. She peeked in the open top of the door and, what luck, saw the buckskin in there. He was sleeping peacefully under his blanket. So, so softly, she nickered.

He flicked an ear and opened his eyes. He was startled to see who it was.

Cloudberry took one look at the simple latch on the door and flipped it open with her lip. Shavings fell out around her feet, but she stepped in. Alidar nickered softly, not believing who it was for a moment, then wondering what she was doing there. Did she come for him?

She cautiously touched nostrils with him, both their necks tensing, and she pulled the blanket off of his hurt leg. It was badly swollen. Gently, she touched her horn to it. Alidar cried out once in pain, but soon his leg felt soothed and didn't hurt anymore. Cloudberry pulled her horn away. The swelling was all gone now, and it should be okay.

She has great healing powers, thought Alidar, moving his leg. He rose to his hooves and the blanket fell off of him. Cloudberry nuzzled him, but she wanted nothing more from him, and she turned to walk out of the stall silently. Alidar was a little disappointed, but that feeling quickly disappeared when he walked on his leg without pain. He closed his door (he was afraid of possums) and plopped back down to sleep. He mustn't go after her. He mustn't scare her away.

Cloudberry was a little tired from healing him, after all, it took a bit of energy, but she was powerful in that way and would be fine the next day. She wandered over and peeked around the trees at Sunridge, who was fast asleep. Then she shied, noticing the shelter on the ground and the two humans just a few feet away from her. Sunridge cocked an ear, but did not seem to wake up. Cloudberry scolded herself for almost letting him know she was there.

Too curious for her own good, she silently approached the shelter and breathed in the human's scent. Why were they sleeping under that bunch of sticks and leaves instead of a house, she wondered? They looked good natured, sleeping there. His mate stirred a little. Of course, she didn't know they were sister and brother.

She suddenly felt a soft muzzle on her shoulder, and whirled around. Sunridge was there. His beautiful white mane looked oddly groomed, and he extended his muzzle hopefully. Cloudberry pinned her ears and backed away, turning to run, but Sunridge cut in front of her challengingly, his own ears going back slightly, as if to say *where do you think you're going, little lady?* She struck at him with a foreleg, and he promptly jumped away, just far enough to keep his over-bearing appearance. He meant business.

But so did Cloudberry. She looked off far behind him. Confused by the lack of attention to him, Sunridge turned his head and looked too.

Cloudberry sprung. Her hooves dug into the ground and she made her strides small to sprint faster. There was a rush of wind and forelock around her ears. Cloudberry accelerated like a race horse, the wind whipping back her mane, chunks of earth flying out behind her. She heard Sunridge taking off as well. She blurred her legs with speed. The wind blinded her but she went into full stride, knowing that she could beat Sunridge's sprint. She was the fastest unicorn in Uni – she could beat Sunridge. She could beat anybody if she really tried, even Smoke Shadow himself couldn't hold a candle to her if she tried hard enough! She told herself this, and she left Sunridge behind, and was a silver streak of moonlight along the black ground, disappearing into the starlit horizon.

Sunridge soon returned glumly, knowing that he was stupid to waste his energy trying to catch her.

The next morning Drake woke up earlier. His watch,

which Lorelei had helped him set for Uni's time, said it was 8:02 am. He had dreamed that Sunridge and the white filly were fighting.

Then he saw the glum look on Sunridge's face, and the deep hoof prints in the ground, and knew it had not been a dream. The white filly had come during the night, and he had missed her!

"What happened?" he asked Sunridge, going to him, with no hesitation, now that he knew he would speak. "With you and the white filly, I mean?"

Sunridge looked at him restlessly. "Well, I tried to catch her but she fooled me and ran off at a million miles an hour. She was over here sniffing around."

"She must have been curious about me," said Drake confidently.

They went over to the house and were surprised to see Valerie sitting on Alidar. Alidar was standing on all four legs. And he was not screeching in pain.

"It's a miracle!" said Nellie.

"Naw, it's the horn," said Alidar. "The white filly came in and healed my leg in the night."

"She came to your stall?" said Nellie suspiciously.

"Yeah, and then she went over to where you guys were." He replied.

"Maybe she's still nearby," said Drake hopefully. It shouldn't take too long to find her this time."

"Well *I'm* not taking you," said Alidar. He and Valerie turned and galloped off into the sunset – err, sunrise.

"Uhhh..." said Nellie, looking at Drake. "Maybe we should wait for her to come back?"

"Not with Sunridge around." Said Drake flatly.

"Then do you expect me to walk for miles out there in the sun, with dragons flying around and evil Nightmare horses and annoying redheaded girls?"

"You don't have to come..."

They had eaten breakfast and were getting ready to go when that dragon from before came again.

"Hi," said Zenny.

"Uhhh... hi," said Drake, looking at him warily.

Zenny went over to the house and knocked. No one answered. Then he came back glumly. "No one's home."

"Say, Zenny, can you run fast?" Nellie asked.

"Sort of."

"Cool, then do you want to come with us to try to make friends with the wild white filly?"

He looked excited. "Sure! Would I ever!"

So they climbed onto Zenny's back, and he ran, on four legs. It felt weird riding a dragon, because he had an arched back and little wings in the way. And he had, not scales, but strange leathery skin that was fiery orange in the sun. And his hobbly gait was very bouncy. *Thank goodness he doesn't have spikes on his back*, thought Drake.

Soon, very soon, Zenny got tired and had to walk. "I'm used to only using two legs," he gasped.

"And you're fat," whispered Nellie evilly. Zenny heard her.

"YOU... YOU THINK I'M FAT," he said, his eyes getting gigantic with tears. "I ONLY TRY NOT TO EAT MEAT AND YET I AM A FAT DRAGON, AND I HAVE HARDLY ANY TEETH, AND TINY WINGS, AND CAN'T BREATHE FIRE! HURT ME, WHY DON'T YOU!"

"Gee, I'm sorry," said Nellie sincerely. "You're not really that fat, and I'm glad you can't bite my arm off."

Zenny was very sensitive, they soon found out, about his appearance. They also found out he was the youngest of his twenty four brothers and sisters, all named starting with the different letters of the alphabet, and he was the smallest and defective. He got picked on and couldn't get a girlfriend.

"Well, that stinks, but look..." said Drake.

The white filly was, once again, up ahead in clear view. She was grazing peacefully. She saw them in an instant and wondered what on earth they were doing riding that dragon.

She recognized him, having seen him before and thankfully, eating some green leaves.

"Hi," called Drake.

The filly eyed them, her eyes widening, then a neigh came from her, and she reared, dancing in place. Then she decided to try something new, and out flapped pearly white wings. She leapt into the air and began to fly upward, then dove down over Zenny.

Zenny tried to fly up after her but his wings were too small to lift his pudgy self. He sunk back down, giving up glumly.

The white filly curled her upper lip at them laughingly, and did a swirl in the air to show off. The three waited on the ground for her to get bored and come down, but instead she gave them an air show and made Zenny very jealous.

It was not until another unicorn that was flying by looked at her strangely that she settled down. She landed and, as if not sure what to do, nickered and pawed. Drake pulled a carrot out of his pocket and called her. "Cloud Filly."

She stopped. Now was time to try! "Hi," she said in an awkward voice, remembering Drake's greeting. She had seen Alidar eat a carrot. She figured it must be good.

Drake bit the carrot and pretended to like it very much. "This is so good. I never want to eat anything else again."

One of the filly's ears was sideways and one was pricked. She was sort of interested. She began walking forward. Then she stopped. She was definitely not coming closer.

Drake held the carrot out, but she stood there with her nose in the air. Drake slid off of Zenny and walked forward. When he got within about ten feet of the filly, she began to back up.

He talked to her.

Bobbing her head, she pawed and then reared again, tucking her nose and tossing her head from side to side. Drake gave up and threw the carrot. It sailed through low air, then rolled to the filly's hooves, and she shied and stared at it, but it was fake fear and soon she was curiously lipping it off the ground and crunching it. She liked it. She nickered and bobbed her head again, craving more of the chewy orange treat. She knew that the boy had some more for her, but he was hiding it somewhere. Maybe in the odd things he was wearing...

Nellie and Zenny watched.

Drake did take out another carrot. He teased her with it, pretending to throw it for her as he did the last one, but holding on to it. The filly thought it flew past her and looked all around, her tail raising, but couldn't find it. Then she saw it still in Drake's hand and stomped a fore hoof at him in annoyance.

"You have to come closer to me to get it," he said.

The filly just looked at him. Suddenly, she reared again, and leapt forward, as if to charge, but skidded to a heavy halt. She backed up quickly again. Drake had jumped back when she did that, and now looked at her smugly.

She thinks she can scare me into giving it to her that easily... he thought.

He broke a piece off of the carrot anyway and threw it, but to less distance. Arching her neck, the filly walked toward it. She was not afraid. After all, she knew she could outrun that birdie-legged thing, but she did not like to be *that* easy. She snatched the carrot and backed up once more.

"You won't even let me pet you?" Drake asked innocently.

She flapped her feathered wings, and hopped a few times. Her humanlike eyes were blue as the sky. Her odd white skin was not translucent or pink like Drake had pictured, but chalk white and soft looking. Her long silvery white mane fell unevenly on both sides of her neck, reaching nearly to her shoulder. It did not appear thick, but it was smooth and unknotted. The filly kept herself clean; obviously she knew she was beautiful.

Drake was holding the last of the carrot and he began nibbling on it. "Nellie, do you want some?" He winked.

"Why, sure Drake," Nellie said walking up and taking some of the carrot. There was laughter in her eyes as she took a nibble.

Drake did not hear the filly come up behind him. Quick as a dash of flash, she reached over his shoulder and, with her lips, snatched the carrot right out of his hand!

"*Hey!*" he shouted as she danced away. "You thief!"

She turned to him and curled her lip again. She had orange all over her mouth now.

"I think she likes you," whispered Zenny, coming to his other side and elbowing Drake with a skinny dragon arm.

Drake tried to make conversation to the filly. "I am Drake, and this is my sister Nellie."

The words ran though her mind. The filly was quickly embarrassed at having thought that Nellie was his mate instead of his sister. She faltered. Turning her head slightly, she folded her wings back in, making them disappear completely and leave her as only a unicorn again.

They looked to one another and waited.

"Come closer, Drake. Pet," said the filly finally.

Drake wasn't hesitant to walk up to her. He could feel her heat and smell her horsy – well, unicorn-y smell. Slowly, he touched her soft white shoulder, still fuzzy from the winter coat of the past cold. (At least this was evidence of Uni being so similar to earth.) His hand brushed her mane. He could barely feel the hairs entwining with his fingers. It was so soft and fine. He wondered if it really was hair, and not a cloud, or something like that.

He was short and she was tall, and he could not see over the top of her back. She was finely built. Her face was very slightly dished, her muzzle small, her nostrils wide at the moment. Drake remembered reading that the Arabs had curved faces, small muzzles, and big nostrils. He wondered if she had it in her blood.

He reached up, unafraid to run his hand along her broad back, making a few short white hairs fly off. He moved his nails and scratched her, and she lipped, enjoying it.

As soon as he'd gotten into it, the filly decided promptly that he'd had enough, and bunched her muscles and suddenly bolted away. Dirt flew all over Drake, but he was too excited to care. It was happy dirt. Spreading her wings out again, the filly flew up over them. She flew so high that she disappeared among the clouds. One day, Drake thought, he would ride her all the way up there, and he would see the cloud unicorns and their clouds.

"Well, are you happy now?" asked Nellie. "You got to

touch her, and now maybe she will look for you instead of the other way around."

"I know she will," said Drake.

Yep, he was right.

Cloudberry wanted to go and find Drake again. She was planning it even as she left them and flew up among the clouds. All was well up there for there were only cumulus clouds, floating through the air like cotton balls with flat bottoms. There would be fine weather tomorrow.

Since the clouds that cloud unicorns lived on looked like large cumulus clouds, she had to do some searching before she finally saw a creamy white horse standing nearly invisible against the white of a cloud unicorn cloud. She circled and landed, bouncing on the soft, yet springy white material, and whinnied a greeting to all.

Horses, foals, yearlings – they all poked their heads out from behind walls of fluff, and up out of the cloud, and looked down from the top. This was a big cloud, housing probably near fifteen cloud unicorns. Cloudberry searched for her mother and old friends, ignoring the interested nickers from the young colts.

Mammatus, her dam, showed herself eventually and nickered a soft greeting. She had a tiny white colt next to her, Cloudberry's little half brother. The father of the colt was the cloud unicorn's herd leader. Only for her and her full blood brother had Mammatus snuck away from the clouds and bred to their ebony black father.

Far away, in the plains near the mountains of Uni there was a great gate of silver and gemstones, white opal and diamond even. The gate, when opened, rather than being a regular gate, sprung open a portal and transported to the other side, which was in the deep darkness of outer space.

On the other side, there were many other gates floating around on their own chunks of land, the entrances to the other sections of Uni, which would otherwise be very difficult to travel to normally. All gates, no matter how scattered, were surrounded by a huge invisible bubble, protecting from the cold and space, and allowing the travelers of the gates to breathe.

In all the starlit blackness, watching over all these gates and portals, there was a black Arab unicorn stallion. He seemed to glisten with the very light of the stars themselves, and his beauty and strength were rivaled by a very small percent. His name was Galaxy Dancer.

He was the gatekeeper, and only he could open the gate's

portals and let the travelers in and out. His job was to help the lost, and to keep Uni pure of bad doings and wicked creatures. He kept watch with royal purple eyes and a strong independence, for the entire population of Uni depended on him. He was so strong and quick, that when the former gatekeeper had gotten too old for the job, he proudly took his place and did a very good job of it.

He was, as said, Arab – though his grandfather was a thoroughbred – but he had met Mammatus while flying around as a young, unneeded Unicorn and they had been close ever since. But she could not live out there in space with him, so whenever she could sneak away from her cloud herd she had gone to see him. First, she had foaled the black colt Nightcloud from him. Then, a few months later, Cloudberry. Cloudberry was white and pearly like her mother, while Nightcloud was black and handsome like his father.

Cloudberry had only once met her father and knew well what he looked like, for a unicorn does not soon forget such a stallion. She liked him, and he was friendly to her, but her brother had always seemed to loathe him for some reason. Nightcloud had said something about how he hated him once when he confronted Cloudberry as a two year old. She never understood. Maybe she never would.

She touched noses with Mammatus and her little colt.

She had not seen them in a few weeks. She had flown down to the ground when she was a yearling (when her wings were fully grown), and preferred to spend her days down there so she could run in the grass. At first she had returned and slept in the clouds every night, but now she rarely did. She was a lone filly, independent and wild in her own world.

"Are you all right still? Are you in a herd? Has Nightcloud bothered you in a while?" Mammatus asked her usual questions.

"I'm fine, I'm not in any herd, and I haven't seen Nightcloud in a long time," she nickered, bored by the questions. "And a human is trying to make friends with me."

"WHAT? Who!? Human? Don't trust them Cloudberry, they're EVIL!" Mammatus said quickly, startling her colt.

"Then why did this one seem so happy and nice to his other unicorn? He even had his sister with him. I learned words from him!" She recited a few words in a meaningless jumble.

Mammatus squealed in shock and covered her foal's ears with her neck. "Be very, very careful around the human and if anything bad happens come up here to the clouds, because they can never get you up here..." she started

"Yeah, yeah."

It was getting late now. After the meeting was over,

Cloudberry flew from the clouds and headed towards the forest. She was going the back way this time. She saw the orange dragon, Zenny, down there walking alone. No humans anymore. She also saw the redheaded girl with her fire horse again. They were down there galloping.

Cloudberry dove down and glided over them. She could fly much faster than that horse could run, and she was sure she could run faster too, if she wanted to try. Songoffire looked up, then whinnied in annoyance because she could not fly after Cloudberry with the saddle on, blocking her wings from flapping out.

Cloudberry landed near the trees and ran into the woods. Here she would wait until dark when Sunridge would be asleep. She was sure he would sleep near the humans, pointing to the pathway of worn grass between the house and the trees in case she tried to come that way again.

There was no breeze this evening in the forest. No one would catch whiff of her smell if she remained calm and quiet.

She came to a stream, pawed, and dropped down to roll in it, accidentally squashing several fish. She had an idea in that unicorn mind of hers. If she got very muddy, then it would mask her scent and brightness and she would blend in with the darkness. She found a muddy place on the edge of the stream and rolled around in it until she was a brown unicorn. Getting dirty was not something she often did, and she did not like the heavy crunchy feeling on her coat. It was a cloud unicorn thing.

She walked through the forest until she could faintly see the back of the human's house. She would remain here until dark, which would not be far off.

She was careful walking around the trees because she didn't want to accidentally ram her horn through one and get stuck. That was the #1 cause of horn loss in Uni, as stated by the Unicorn section government. The unicorns lived a dangerous life.

Cloudberry was spying on the back of the house when suddenly someone nickered from behind. Cloudberry jumped and whirled around, surprised. Sunridge? No. The buckskin she had healed was there. His black horn seemed to glint green like his eyes. Cloudberry recognized him and nickered, her heart still going at a million miles an hour. The buckskin, Alidar of course, quickly recognized her through the mud because of her long legs and the white skin on her muzzle.

"I didn't hear you come up!" The filly whickered.

"I did not want you to." He replied.

Cloudberry looked suspicious "Were you stalking me?"

"No, No! I was just pooping in the woods, I swear," Alidar

said quickly, before she got angry and screamed or some filly-ish thing like that. Instead she looked grossed out. He needed to change the subject. He was NOT being very smooth.

"Why are you all dirty?" he asked curiously.

"I don't want Sunridge to see me."

"He's still out there grazing with the herd. They haven't come into the woods yet."

"It won't be long... is... Drake there?"

"Yes..." Alidar squinted. "He said you let him pet you."

"I didn't mind."

"Do you want the humans to own you?"

"No one can own me. But we can be friends."

"That's what you might think. But then they'll just ride you everywhere and never let you leave."

"But you're out here walking around free. You don't leave."

"Yes, but some people keep their unicorns in stalls all day, Filly..."

"I can open a stall if I want. Besides, Drake would not do that because he has no place to keep me anyway, does he?"

"He will someday. He will move and get a house built."

"I'll tell him that I won't leave. I never lie."

"Well... why are you even so curious about the humans when other unicorns are afraid of them?"

"Because life needs some pep... it's not just eating grass all day. What if I like being ridden? Maybe I'll even be a racehorse."

"What if you become a *dressage* horse instead!?"

"Dressage? I couldn't ever do any of that fancy dancing or anything."

Alidar sighed. She was a lost cause. Well, no one could say he hadn't tried to warn her.

"If you want, I can tell Drake you're out here and he can come to see you. That way you don't have to meet him looking like that," he offered, thinking her muddy exterior only made her look rougher. "Oh, and by the way, my name is Alidar."

She nodded, keeping her own name to herself. "Yes... but that takes the fun out of daringly appearing like a shaft of moonlight and I want to see more of how the humans live."

"You are insane!" Alidar snorted softly.

"You are too grumpy and depressing!" She strutted back off into the woods. She was going to roll until the mud came off of her and she blew everyone's mind with beauty.

Alidar snorted and strutted off in the other direction. He only looked back over his shoulder twice.

"Well, you sure look P.Oed about something," Valerie said five minutes later when she saw Alidar. "Are you constipated?" she whispered.

"NO, I AM NOT CONSTIPATED!"

Drake and Nellie looked at him funny.

Lorelei came out the house with Noopie following. Alidar noticed a fat chestnut pinto horse standing outside. Lorelei took some lotion and smeared it on the horse's pink sunburned muzzle.

"That should help with your burning," she said. The horse nickered thankfully and left.

"Hey, that was MY hand lotion that you just used on that horse!" said Valerie. "Can't you just get your own stuff or something?"

"Well I don't often use that girly stuff," Lorelei said. "And it's my job to help animals. And you need to help too!"

"I do help!"

"But not enough!"

There was a big glaring contest.

"Witch fight," said Drake, nudging Nellie in the side.

Soon it was dinnertime and Nellie and Drake went into the kitchen to get food.

"You need to get money and buy your own food," growled Lorelei. "Or I'll start using my secret evil sorceress ingredients."

"Ehh... we will, as soon as I can ride the filly and win a race with her. We'll pay you back real good.

"How do you know you'll even get to ride her? What if you never see her again? Maybe she's met a stallion and going to be a fat broodmare."

"I guarantee I'll see her again AND ride her or I'll eat Alidar."

Alidar choked on a carrot.

"But she really could be in foal," said Nellie, raising her eyebrow.

"Well... she seems to keep away from the other horses, so I would doubt it."

"It is springtime... she might have mated with a stallion and then left him."

"I'd guess she only just turned three though."

"Okay, stop talking about that at the table!" Alidar was poking his head in the window as usual. "Everyone's talking about, well, *that* stuff and not giving me food!"

"Right," said Valerie, embarrassed.

"How old are you Alidar?" asked Nellie.

"I am a 4 year old stallion," he said.

"I thought you had to be at least five to be a real stallion." said Nellie. "You're still a little colt."

Alidar snorted on Nellie's food. "I will turn five this autumn!" he said.

Drake was poking at a strange piece of food on his plate when he heard a squeal from Alidar. He saw him pull his head out of the window and heard him nicker something irritably. There was no mistaking the flash of bright white behind him.

"Drake! Your filly bit me!" the buckskin tattled.

Bravely, the filly looked in the window, her muzzle almost resting on the sill. She shied away when Drake and Nellie came over to poke their heads out, but then pranced back. She arched her neck and nickered.

"Now that's a gorgeous horse!" said Valerie, seeing her.

A light seemed to radiate from the prancing filly. She tossed back her long forelock. Her small, perfect hooves were clean and tan-colored, and well worn from galloping. Here she was, showing off for all too see, not the least bit afraid of the humans she knew she could outrun.

Alidar was distraught. Everyone loved the filly! And he was swept aside while she danced for attention. But he was most hurt by Valerie's exclamation of "now that's a gorgeous horse!"

He began to dance like the filly. He did an extended trot, then lifted his forefeet of the ground and hopped. He did a spin on his hindquarters and then a rollback. Then he did the moonwalk and the robot. Now everyone was watching him.

He stopped and bowed. But he lost his balance and fell over.

Everyone laughed. The filly came over and nudged him up. Alidar blushed madly, a pink tinge showing beneath his hairs.

No one had noticed Drake going out the back door and walking towards the filly.

"Hi," she said, noticing him. She waited for him with one forefoot raised and her head up high.

"She's not anything like a regular wild unicorn," Lorelei said. "Are you sure she hasn't just escaped from an old owner?"

"She did not know a word of human language when I first saw her. She neighed. A tame unicorn would know how to talk."

Drake stroked her soft shoulder, and felt it was a little damp. She had gotten wet –swam – before she came!

Nellie followed Drake out and the filly eyed her curiously. She smelled her on the wind, and she smelled clean and sweet. Drake put his hand out and the filly put her muzzle on it. Never had there been a time when he wished more for a carrot!

Her muzzle was fuzzy and whiskery, yet her odd skin felt soft as a model's. Her horn was white, but shone like silver in an odd way.

Nellie greeted the filly and touched her smooth hide. She was so soft and warm it was as if she was a cloud herself... now she knew why they called them cloud unicorns. She wondered what they looked like when they got their colorful spots from the rain.

Suddenly, as Valerie and Lorelei approached, she decided it was time for her to go. She cantered around the house and galloped away like a wild mare, seeming not as awkward and long as she had before. Sunridge stood with his rump to a tree, now having the herd in the forest again. He dozed, and as he did, the filly went by so silently that he wondered if he was dreaming or not.

The humans and Alidar stood there watching her go. She skidded to a stop at the top of a hill bare of trees, already about a quarter of a mile away. She stood against the horizon, and as the sunset, there were sunrays reaching out into space from a swelling cumulus cloud, and the filly seemed to have a golden lining from the sunlight. She reared once and whinnied.

Sunridge was nearby watching, he was awake now. He thought he was dreaming. He saw the heavenly filly there, all outlined in silver and gold, but he did not believe she was real. She seemed to dance on the horizon and the sunrays, then she disappeared, over the side of the hill, or did she simply fade into the clouds...?

Chapter 5

Now Drake's Filly

Drake did not have to go far the next day. He walked out in the early morning and called. The filly had not gone far at all. She appeared happily over the hill. She had to play hard to get, at least a little, so she didn't come until he held an apple slice out for her.

"Hi Drake," she said in her pretty young female voice. It was funny that she could make the words so perfectly in her odd horse mouth. "Us friends," she said, more to herself to forget that negative talking Alidar.

"Yes," Drake said. The filly nuzzled him and galloped around, showing off. He did not want to wait. He wanted to ride her soon.

Drake just called her again, and she followed him. They went back to Lorelei's house.

The filly froze when she saw Sunridge looking at her, but he knew that she belonged to Drake now. Or did she? She didn't want to belong to anyone. Drake would never be superior to her.

Valerie rode by on Alidar. Alidar gave the filly a look.

"Oh, so she's friends with you now," Valerie commented, stopping her mount and looking at both of them. "Can you ride her, Drake?"

"That's a good question." Drake turned to the filly. "Can I ride you?"

She bobbed her head, as if deciding. She moved sideways a bit, and her barrel bumped into Drake's back.

Drake tried to get on, but she was too tall for him to mount from the ground. Realizing this, she walked over to a rock, nickering, and he managed to get on her back from there. He kicked a leg over to her other side and pushed himself up to a normal position. All right! Now he was finally sitting on his horse!

The filly bobbed her head and twitched her skin at the odd weight. Her hooves shifted. She did not want to buck her new friend off, but it felt awfully strange, and he was up there where she couldn't see him unless she looked around. She walked forward and it took a few steps for her to get balanced. Even though Drake had a death grip on her mane, he tried to help her by sitting up straighter.

Valerie couldn't help but grin. "Well then. Do you guys wanna race?" She winked. She didn't expect Drake to say yes.

But this was what Drake had been waiting for. "Yes!" he said, of course. Cloudberry could run the legs off of that little Alidar!

The filly seemed to know, and she got excited and pranced to the side of Alidar, who didn't look quite as energetic. Drake bounced unprofessionally. He did not have any idea how he would stop the filly or control her in any way, but he would get to race!

Valerie tried to hide her surprise. She hoped Drake didn't get himself killed… "Are you ready? All right… on your mark… get set… … gallop!"

The filly was surprised, learning the words, and for a moment she let Alidar sprint off and ahead of her. Then she exploded after him, Drake hanging on to her mane, feeling his hands slide back, his legs slide back, and just slide back completely. Knowing he'd lost his balance, he kicked his legs forward, trying desperately not to slip back anymore. How would it look if he fell straight off the back of her rump?

He leaned forward, like a jockey, as the filly broke into a large, swinging gallop and pursued madly after Alidar, moving faster and faster with every gigantic stride. Truly running now, she seemed to leap through the air, her legs barely touching the ground before she shot off again! She was quickly catching Alidar, then she blew past him, and she was running alone, leaving him behind.

She galloped on joyfully until she could not hear him behind her anymore. She slowed reluctantly, Drake gripping with his legs unprofessionally and leaning back, coaxing her to go back to where Valerie and Alidar were.

"We won, girl, we won our first race!"

"Easy," said the filly proudly, as they curved in a bouncy arc back to their 'competitors', who had slowed to a stop.

"Man, she's definitely fast," sad Valerie, amazed. "Maybe you're not such a fool to want to race her. She runs like a thoroughbred... and maybe not even like a thoroughbred," she said.

Alidar looked put down. Seeing this, the barely exerted filly nuzzled him on the neck. He turned his head away. It wasn't his fault he was small and slow....

It was then that they saw Nellie come running across the grass to them. "Drake!" She shrieked. "When did the filly let you ride her? Did you gallop?"

"We just happened to outrun Valerie and Alidar," said Drake, triumphantly, glancing at them for their reaction.

Valerie rolled her eyes. "Ahh, we could have beat ya if we really tried," she patted Alidar. "Speaking of beat, we'll go back now, bye." She and Alidar turned to trot away. They were over it.

"I want to ride too," Nellie said, looking up at Drake. "You will let me ride you, won't you?"

The filly bobbed her head as an obvious yes.

"I suppose." Drake grumbled.

Nellie jumped on her much more gracefully than Drake had. The filly sunk with the sudden weight of two humans on her back. She walked across the grass, grunting.

They walked for a while, until they had made a loop and were back near Lorelei's house again. Then the filly knew that she had had enough, and stopped stubbornly. She looked around at them in annoyance. The humans sighed and slid off.

Drake was happy that he had at least gotten to ride her, and he pulled the rest of his apple out of his pocket and gave it to her.

"Hmm… I think I'll call you Cloudy," Drake suggested. Nellie groaned with the use of a boring name.

The filly shook her head. "No!" She wanted to tell him her real name, Cloudberry, but she did not know "berry." She couldn't tell him properly, he'd think her name was Cloud…

"Uhhh… Skye?" Drake guessed.

"No!"

"Whitney?"

"Neeeigh!"

"Cream? Silver? Bob?"

She looked at him in disgust, her lip twitching.

"Okay then, I'll just call you The Filly until you can say your name," he said.

The filly snorted.

"But I hope I know it by the time you're a champion race-horse," Drake said confidently.

"Racehorse!" Cloudberry said.

"Yes, The Filly. Don't you want to become a great race-horse?" he suggested eagerly.

"Yes!" The filly bobbed her head excitedly. She had flown over racetracks before. From a distance, thought rac-ing looked fun. She had never noticed the whips or the loud noise, only the happy unicorn or horse in the winner's circle standing proudly.

"Then we must train every day and get in shape... and you have to learn to wear a saddle and bridle."

The filly put one ear back and one ear forward and gave him the upper lip.

For the rest of that day they all walked around in the woods because the filly was tired of being ridden and, for once, she wanted to roll. Just to get that feeling off! Nellie and Drake were pleased that she trusted them enough to roll when they were there, because unicorns and horses usually didn't roll if there was danger there.

She grunted and rested there on the ground for a few minutes after she did so, and then she got up and shook. White hairs flew everywhere. She was still shedding from the winter hair she had grown before.

Drake and Nellie took pinecones and scratched her back. It felt really good to her. She arched her neck and lipped. She liked to lip, as you can see.

They got tired of scratching finally and it was surprisingly late, Drake noticed. Soon it would be dinnertime. The filly hadn't done much grazing, and now she was quite hungry. She began to crop grass hastily.

Nellie left soon, because she was hungry as well and she knew Drake liked to be alone with his horse. And he did, so he stayed with the filly for a few minutes, then left.

"I will stay in the forest here," the filly said as he walked away.

"Then I'll come back after I eat, said Drake. He disappeared among the trees.

The filly grazed contentedly. She thought, while she grazed, about Drake's plans for her. She didn't mind being a racehorse, but she didn't want to wear one of those ugly saddles. She didn't mind being ridden by him, but he *and* his sister were too heavy. She wondered how little Alidar did it.

She wondered if she would ever be a famous unicorn and she wondered if she would ever have a mate. She wanted to have foals one day, but after she was done with everything else in her life. She wondered if her brother would ever return, and if he would try to fight her. Why did he hate her? Was it because their mother had never let him near her after Cloudberry was born? Cloudberry had never been mean to him, ever, even when he nipped and kicked at her when she came over to see what he was doing.

The filly suddenly got an idea. *I must find berries,* she thought in her horsy mind. Drake would ask her about the berries, and she would know the word, and she could say her name, CLOUDBERRY! It was amazing how unicorns quickly learned words.

She trotted through the woods, but there were no berries. She would have to go up to the clouds and get a cloud berry.

And she did, stretching her neck towards the sky and beating her feathery wings.

She landed gracefully on a cloud, a cloud that she saw a cloud colt standing on. She ignored the colt, who was nickering hopefully at her, and went into a hole in the side of the whiteness.

Here, there were a few mares and foals. All white with white skin, the same as she. There were many patches of cloud berries nearby, and standing crystal clear in a corner, there was a rain pool to drink out of. This space inside of the cloud was dome-shaped, just enough sunlight coming through to keep the unicorn's eyes adjusted.

The filly – well I guess you could call her Cloudberry now instead of switching between the filly and Cloudberry randomly – bowed her head respectively to the others, ones she did not know, and quickly picked up a plant with one large red berry on it. Carrying it by the green stem, she left, the rejected cloud colt whinnying after her.

The cloud berries ranged in color from light pink to deep red. Cloudberry liked the red ones the best. The pink ones were too bland, loved the most by the foals and yearlings. A cloud berry was a cloud unicorn's typical diet up there. They didn't have a lot of protein, but they were juicy, and gave energy. Cloud unicorns were not often very strong or chunky because of this. They were always lean and slim. A cloud berry was usually the size of a golf ball.

After gliding back down with the wind whipping even more loose white hairs out of her coat, Cloudberry landed and galloped through the forest until she reached the place where she had been grazing, just before Drake returned from his dinner, burping. She raised her head and quickly came over, the berry's plant hanging from her mouth.

"What's this... a big berry?"

When he said 'berry', she was able to put two and two together. "NAME! NAME! CLOUDBERRY!" she said excitedly, bobbing her head.

Drake seemed to get the message. "That's your name? Cloudberry? Cool!"

Cloudberry dropped the odd plant on his head, and he caught it as it fell off.

"Am I supposed to eat it?" He eyed it warily. *What if she dropped it in dirt by accident or somebody licked it or it's for unicorns only and poisonous to humans?* He thought.

Cloudberry nickered and grabbed the stem of it. She pulled it away and Drake ended up with just the berry in his hands. He sniffed it.

Cloudberry just looked at him while she munched on the green stem.

"Drake what are you doing?"

Drake jumped and turned around. There was Valerie. Again.

"Are you going to sleep over here now? Next to your wonderful dream filly?" she teased.

"Her name is Cloudberry, and she's my *friend*," he said. "I'd rather be near her than boring ol' Sunridge." Then he added in a whisper, "Are these berries poisonous?"

"No, you dummy! You're too cautious! Gimme that!" She snatched the berry from him with pink-finger nailed hands, and bit off half of it. Cloudberry pricked her ears, wondering what Drake would do.

"It's delicious." she said, handing him the rest. Drake took it and munched it embarrassedly. "This is better than chocolate!" he soon said, his eyes lighting up.

Cloudberry tossed her forelock. She preferred grass, but she liked seeing the boy relishing the berry. The berry that SHE had given him.

"So you figured out her name," Valerie said. "I guess she's really yours now… poor Alidar has been worrying about it for some reason now. You know, I think he likes her."

"Well, he's got good taste, but I don't think it would work out between them," Drake said, looking around. "He's a bit small…"

"Yeah, but now that Cloudberry is friends with you, he seems to think you're going to go away and take her with you."

"I don't think we'll leave this place anytime soon," Drake said. "We don't have any money to build a house or anything."

"Are you ever going to get a job? The world here isn't so different from your world, you know."

"No, I'm going to become a jockey and race Cloudberry. We'll win big."

"You have to be fifteen to get your jockey license."

"I am fifteen."

"But you don't hardly know how to ride! All you can do is hang on. I bet you'd wreak havoc with a bit."

"I can learn, I just need a saddle!"

"And you need money to buy a saddle!"

"But you have a saddle, don't you?" Drake asked slyly.

"Well, yes..." she lowered her eyebrows. "but it's probably too small for the filly, and it's an English saddle, not a racing saddle."

"So? They're not that different, are they?"

"The only kind of races you could enter with an English saddle, longer stirrups and no jockey license are little cheap races for unprofessional riders and unregistered racehorses. And you can only win about $50 with those."

"But we'd still get money!" Drake reasoned. "And while

we did that I could save up and buy racing tack and get a jockey license!"

Valerie sighed. "So bent on things…" she said, walking away.

As she left, Nellie came. "What were you doing with *her*, Drake?" she asked teasingly.

"We were just discussing my jockey license," Drake said.

The next morning Nellie woke up before everyone as always. She looked at Drake's watch. It was almost 9:00 am. He was drooling.

Cloudberry was grazing around. They all sat there peacefully, when Valerie appeared AGAIN, with Alidar following. She had some papers in her hand.

"Drake! Drake wake up!"

"Huh?" Drake said groggily.

"I've got papers on horse racing!"

Nellie and Drake looked, and Cloudberry came over and tried to look but there was no room and she couldn't read. The first paper said:

Uni Racing Association Rules

1. The jockey riding must be at least 15, have a jockey license, and wear silks. All jockeys must be less than 5'7 and weigh no more than 115 pounds.

2. The horse must be registered as a <u>racehorse</u>. Any horse can be a racehorse if it fits the description, which is over 14 hands, over two years old, not have history of bad injury, and be willing to race.

Drake's confidence grew as he read on. There were more rules, but he wouldn't break any of them. He could register Cloudberry as a racehorse and become a jockey as soon as he got his license. The rules here were different than the ones he knew.

"And here's the rules for getting your jockey license," Valerie said, showing another paper.

Getting a Jockey License

If one is to become a jockey they must have a license so they can be identified. The person must be at least fifteen and pass a test to see how well they can handle an excited horse or unicorn. The person seeking license must have their parents or some other dependable person to reinforce their information.

That was the only stuff on the page that Drake paid any mind. His parents weren't there to say he was fifteen... hey maybe he could bribe two old people to pretend to be his parents!

"It seems possible that you could be a jockey if you really wanted to," Valerie said smugly. "But your parents aren't here to say you're fifteen, and you don't exactly look too old."

"I could find a way."

"And you're not even really fifteen are you?"

"I am. But even if I wasn't, no one here knows me. I came from another planet, I think."

"Pffff... well you STILL need your parents!"

"I'll win 50 bucks in a little unofficial race and bribe two old people to dress up as my parents."

"Hey! I want 50 bucks!" Valerie jumped.

"You're NOT my parents!"

"But I've got a magic wand."

"I thought you were against me being a jockey!"

"I never said that!"

Drake narrowed his eyes at her.

She went "Humph" and turned. "If you don't want my help, then I won't help you!" She marched off.

"Weird crazy mumble, mumble, mumble..." Drake growled and mumbled.

Nellie elbowed him. "I think she was trying to flirt with you," she hinted.

Drake kept mumbling and went over to Cloudberry, looking at her happily when he saw her.

"C'mon, Cloudberry, let's go for another ride."

He failed to jump on her, so he ended up climbing her mane. She sunk sideways, her ears going back in unappreciativeness.

Surprisingly strong hair for being so soft, thought Drake.

"What about me?" Nellie said.

"Two is too heavy," Cloudberry said earnestly.

"You're not even as strong as Alidar!"

They trotted off before she could say anything else.

Cloudberry had a nice, long, slow stride when she trots, so she was very smooth. Drake was brave enough not to hold the mane for a moment but then she started going fast and he accidentally dug his heels into her sides.

Her head shot up and she flew forward. Drake flew *backward* – right off her behind. Just as he had tried so hard not to do the day before.

She was bucking madly, her sides itching, and then she figured out he was off, so she came back curiously. "When did you go down there?"

Drake did not want her to know that he had fallen off in a very unprofessional way, so he said that she bucked him off. "Please don't ever buck, Cloudberry, it's very bad," he said. "For my health."

"Don't kick my sides, then." she said. "It's bad for my health."

He got back on her again. He was getting better at it. "When I tell you to whoa, whoa – I mean stop."

"Why whoa and not stop?"

"Because that's the way it is. Ask the cowboys."

"What cowboys? Are they hiding in the bushes!?" She spooked madly at a bird. Drake went flying off again.

Cloudberry got over her fears quickly. She came back

over to Drake who was lying there in the grass. "You don't know how to ride, do you?"

"What are you talking about? I've ridden before."

Cloudberry curled her lip at him.

"Don't you give me that! I can ride perfectly fine… stop that!"

She waited for him to get back on again, but he didn't, so she started to graze. Drake decided that he needed to borrow that saddle and bridle from Valerie. This was going to be complicated.

Cloudberry had a nice, wide chest with a strong, muscular shoulder. From where her mane ended to the point, it sloped. He had read that this was good conformation. Her back was pretty short and her tail wasn't too high on her rump. He also noticed that her back legs weren't bent as much as Alidar's were. They were rather straight, and her hocks were high. Of course, she was still young and gawky, and her rump was higher than her withers, but that would even out when she was older. She had very strong looking hindquarters and wide hips.

Random conformation evaluation. Okay it was time to get back on her…

Drake tried as hard as he could to sound logical. "Trot

means trot, canter means canter, and the kissy noise means to gallop fast. Whoa means to stop. Got it?"

"Huh?" Cloudberry did not get it. "What's a canter?"

"Oh, yeah. I forgot you didn't know those words yet."

Drake had to tell her what everything meant.

"A canter is when I'm doing a really slow gallop?"

"Yes. Or a lope if you're western."

"A lope?"

Drake groaned as he explained some more. Finally Cloudberry understood what everything meant... except sometimes she tried to read Drake's mind, which always said gallop, and took off madly before he could finish saying *canter*. But Drake let her get away with it since he loved to gallop – the gallop wasn't bumpy like her canter was. But that was okay because she sprung on her hindquarters well – and Drake liked to ride her while she was feeling so powerful. The only thing he *didn't* like about her was her withers. *I need a strap-on saddle pad or something...* he thought worriedly.

Soon he looked at his watch and saw that it had been three hours. He was hungry and tired and sore. Cloudberry was in better shape, but she was blowing and sweating so much that Drake thought he might slide off. She had a lot of stamina, he thought positively. He hoped he hadn't pushed her – yet, it had seemed, somewhat that she was the one pushing him? He was breathing pretty hard himself.

Lunch was ready back at Lorelei's. Drake patted Cloudberry and promised he would give her an apple AND a carrot when he got back from lunch. Nellie was a little annoyed at him for leaving her.

"I had to sit here all morning reading that book of unicorns and things! Now I want a black Arabian unicorn instead of a Friesian! I hope you're happy!"

Drake knew she was just complaining for the sake of complaining. But nothing could get his spirits down now; he HAD A HORSE! Or better yet... A UNICORN!

He appeared in the house humming Britney Spears songs happily, and Valerie looked at him strangely and he switched over to some more manly songs.

As said before, but just to remind you, there was a TV on the wall in the cramped living room/oversized closet. Lorelei had it turned on and was watching unicorn racing.

Drake came and sat down and stared with interest. He hadn't seen unicorns racing yet. There was a nice aerial view of the track. It was regular oval (well almost) shaped.

The camera went to the horses, which were post parading. There were nine horses, mostly thoroughbreds, some with horns, and then there was a gray Arab-looking unicorn and a brown one who was quite stocky and had a shiny red horn, like a long pointy ruby.

"That stocky one doesn't look like it'll last long," said Drake.

"The race is only six furlongs." Lorelei was eating a baloney sandwich with... was it sherbet ice cream? Drake twisted his lip.

The race's stats came on. It was the Silver Spoon Juvenile Sprint. It was indeed six furlongs. The purse was – Drake gulped – quite, quite high. He only had to win one of those races to be rich.

The favorite of the race was a tall bay thoroughbred. He didn't have a horn, but he had a pretty, wide blaze and one white sock on his right front leg. His jockey was wearing turquoise silks with an orange dot in the middle, and it went well with the horse's brown, Drake thought.

"Can they still talk and stuff if they don't have a horn?" he asked Lorelei.

She provided this answer for the second time. "Sure. But I think horns help the unicorns to learn language and stuff better. It has nothing to do with how smart they are, but horns are magical, so... they can almost read your mind. And they can also stab stuff and heal stuff."

"Cloudberry healed Alidar's leg," said Drake. "She must be a healing unicorn and not a stabbing unicorn."

The jockeys in the race were all regular looking. They were short guys in big mushroom helmets and funny outfits and goggles. The only difference between these jockeys and the ones he knew, were the horses. The mounts of theirs walked calmly, proudly, and smoothly. Of course they knew what everything around them was and some of them were even challenging each other. Only some of the jockeys carried a crop.

"Why do those jockeys carry crops when they could just tell the horses to go?" Drake wondered aloud.

"There are some horses that need extra encouragement," Lorelei said, shrugging. "And some guys are just mean. That's why racehorses don't usually make friends with their jockeys."

"Cloudberry doesn't need to be cropped," Drake said confidently. The filly loved to run, and it was because of that that she was so fast and so in shape.

The horses loaded into the gate. A few seconds later the bell rang, and they all came exploding out. The stocky one, to Drake's surprise, out sprinted all the others. But it slowed when it was in front, and dropped back to fifth place. The favorite took the lead.

"It's Flickerfire in the lead now... Mud Ruby has dropped back and in second is Zasha..." The announcer had a weird accent, and he made his A's sound like O's.

The positions didn't change much during the race except for a chestnut horse falling behind. The jockeys all started urging their horses on as they came near a quarter of a mile of race left. Flickerfire, the favorite, increased his lead. But there was Mud Ruby, brown legs a blur, beginning to catch him!

The gray Arab didn't look tired but he simply wasn't going fast enough. He was in fourth place. Reaching down in a quick movement, the jock flicked the crop across his shoulder. The gray shot forward, but only to be passed by a brown unicorn with three white socks as they went under the wire.

Drake hadn't seen who had won because he was watching the Arab. "Who...?"

"Mud Ruby couldn't catch him!" Nellie said.

They showed a picture of the finish with Flickerfire's neck in front as they went under the wire. Then there was Flickerfire's trainer, gloaty and proud, saying that he knew he would win because the track was a tad muddy. "He doesn't mind a bit of suction under his 'ooves at all, now." Came from the speakers.

Flickerfire was taken to the winner's circle and awarded with a little silver spoon. The jockey held it up triumphantly.

"I wish I could do that," said Drake with envy. Then he got an idea. "Hey, if that redhead girl we met really *is* a jockey, maybe she can help me." he said. She hadn't appeared to have any parents around, come to think of it...

He ate lunch (baloney sandwich with too much mayonnaise courtesy of Valerie) and grabbed an apple and a carrot from the stash of horse treats that Lorelei could make to magically refill itself. She hid it in the corner because Alidar would see and sneak into the house and spend all day there.

Cloudberry was napping, with her lower lip drooping, when he came back. Drake took a blade of grass and tickled her side with it softly out of sheer curiosity of what would happen. Cloudberry's skin twitched and she lipped.

He went over and flapped her lip with his finger.

"Drake are you bonding with her?" Nellie appeared and asked in his ear. He jumped, and Cloudberry woke and jumped too. Nellie snickered.

"Aww you su..." he started to say. Cloudberry put her chin on his head. She had some long whiskers.

Nellie pushed Drake over and started walking off into

the forest. She had on the yellow dress of her arrival in Uni again. She had kept it, since it reminded her of her home. Her long, black and curly hair was shining. Thank goodness Valerie and Lorelei's house had a shower on the side of it... Drake didn't trust the fish in that stream!

"Sisters are so annoying," he said to Cloudberry.

"Brothers too," she said, agreeing. "And mean."

"I'm not mean... am I?" Drake said, thinking she was referring to him.

"No but there's a mean guy who lives near here."

"Is he like an evil wizard guy who wants to destroy all unicorns or take over the planet or something like that?" Drake was nervous. He had been watching too many movies.

"No he's just mean. He throws hard brown things at me and is mean to his..." she didn't know 'dragon' or 'rocks' yet.

Drake was thinking of some very disturbed things in his very disturbed mind. Did he throw poop at her and be mean to his wife? Or did he throw rocks at her and be mean to his horse? Or did he throw coconuts and be mean to his giraffe? The last one was unlikely, Drake decided.

"Is it rocks that he throws?" he asked fearfully.

"Uhhh... yes!"

"And is he mean to his wife?"

"No, he has no mate… he rides it… it's blue… it's not a unicorn either."

"His dragon!"

"Yes!"

"So he's just a mean guy who throws rocks at you and has a dragon. No trench coat or shades or anything?"

"I do not think so."

Soon after Drake had given Cloudberry her treats they needed something to do so they went walking through the forest and caught up with Nellie. They knew it real well now, but Nellie the most. She had been walking around it every morning since Drake was riding and she had nothing to do. Maybe, she thought, she'd play a trick on Drake.

They weaved around the trees, and soon they came to the stream. Cloudberry, who was following Drake, dipped her muzzle in it and scared the fish.

"Drake I found the coolest thing the other day," Nellie said.

"What? Was it worth money?"

"I dunno. I wasn't strong enough to pick it up. But you have to see it!"

Drake followed her even deeper into the forest, unaware, of course, that it was all a trick. Nellie had to keep from laughing. She bit her tongue.

"What did the thing look like? Was it shiny?" Drake asked.

"I can't describe it, but it was definitely awesome. No, it's not a portal that will transport us to another unknown foreign land if we touch it. I learned that already."

Pretty soon the cups of purple soda that Drake had drunk ran through him and he had to "go do something." So Nellie and Cloudberry waited there while he disappeared into the woods.

Nellie brought Cloudberry's head close to her and whispered into her ear. Cloudberry began to giggle, something she had picked up from Valerie. They both sat there giggling evilly.

"Don't forget, Drake can't know what we're doing, so keep quiet," Nellie whispered as she heard Drake coming back.

"Hi everybody," he said nervously as he saw them giggling madly. They began walking away so he looked fearfully to see if his pants were unzipped but they weren't, thank goodness.

Females, he thought in annoyance. *I hope Cloudberry doesn't form some sort of secret affiliation with Nellie because they're girls and I'm a guy. Maybe I should have gotten a colt... no, then he would think I was queer every time I hugged him or something...*

"Are we very close to the thing?" Drake asked Nellie after another minute.

"Yeah, almost. It's right up here."

Soon they came to a larger hill than Drake had seen so far, with a steep cliff edge sticking up like a limestone wall. There was a cave in the side, and there was sand around it so it looked well used. Cloudberry knew the cave. She had gone through it once. It had tunnels going through to the top of the cliff. There were a few of them, but they weren't too hard to follow. If you got lost you would find your way out within 30 minutes. Lots of horses and unicorns and other assorted magical animals used the main cave as a way up to the top of the cliff.

Drake did not know that, though. "Nellie…" he said. "Are you sure there isn't some sort of evil creature in there that'll kill the snot out of us if we go into its house?"

"It's fine." she said. "Follow me."

They stepped into the cave, and went through the darkness a little ways. Nellie had her hands out in front of her and felt something. "Watch out for the…"

"OW!!" Drake ran smack-dab into the randomly grown stalactite. He growled. "Stupid random stalactite…"

He tried to walk on, but accidentally kicked the not-quite-as-random stalagmite right under it.

"OW!! SON OF A…"

The females snickered. Drake glared and made Cloudberry go ahead of him. She easily evaded the painful cave formations and Drake followed her. It was pitch black so he held onto her silky tail, which seemed to glow in the darkness, it was so white. Of course she didn't really glow, but she was visible.

They walked for a long while and soon Drake let go of Cloudberry's tail and lagged behind. Maybe it was all a lie.…

"Okay Nellie, your cruel joke must end now… hey where are you?"

Drake hadn't seen Nellie silently go into another tunnel that was on the side of the one they were traveling on. And Cloudberry had done the same with another as soon as he had let go. Now he was alone and wondering.

"Hello… where'd you guys go? I'm lost… aagh! You dirtbags!" Drake realized he'd been tricked.

Chapter 6

So you want to be a Jockey...

Nellie laughed to herself as she followed her tunnel. She could hear Drake's faint cursing in the distance... it sounded eerie with all the echoing. She must get out of this cave... it was too dark and wet and scary. Her tunnel went slightly upward, so she knew she was going to the top of the cliff. She would wait there for Cloudberry and Drake.

Cloudberry knew her tunnel was taking her to the low side of the cliff. She would fly to the top like Nellie had said to do and they would meet Drake there when he found his way out. Muahahahaha, to scare Drake!

Drake was walking along trying to find the way out and cursing himself for being dumb. He stopped to rest and sat down... right on a small but terribly painful stalagmite.

"OWWWWCH!" Drake jumped up, rubbing his rear. And of course he nearly stabbed himself to death on the stalactite above but he jumped at an angle so it only ripped his shirt off. So now Drake was angry and lost and shirtless in a cave.

Being shirtless made him feel very vulnerable and he

walked around hunched up like a really constipated person trying to avoid the random stalactites and stalagmites.

Suddenly, he saw light. There was a hole in the ceiling! He ran over to it, luckily not hitting anything, and groaned when he reached the lighted spot and saw that he still had a long way up to go. The light was very small.

He looked down. He noticed a rock sticking out of the wall, lit up by the light coming from the ceiling. Actually it was a large gem, not a rock. It was at least a square foot. He noticed that there were some smaller ones, too. None of them were above four inches, though.

The gem shone oddly. It was a sort of metallic gray. Not silver, but just gray. He looked into it. With the light, it was like a mirror... but it reflected him with gray skin and darker gray hair. It was like an old TV/mirror, sort of...

It was then that he felt an odd chill and in the reflection he could see the body of a gray horse passing behind him. He turned, but he saw nothing. Puzzled, he looked back in. Now, there was a gray horse standing behind him looking in also.

He turned again to look at it, and there was nothing. He could feel nothing. He glanced again into the gem and saw that, in the reflection, his hand was on the horse's face. He took it off quickly and looked at it. It had an odd gray powder on it.

He looked closer into the gem and the horse was still there. In fact it looked kind of P.Oed that he had touched it. The horse scared Drake... he didn't quite know why until he noticed that its eyes were like black holes, not shining – only black. And its breath breathed icy cold on his back.

He knew it was there. It was right there, somehow. His heartbeat quickened only about a kazillion times faster. Terrified, he couldn't move as he saw it slowly float away from him in the gem. Then he seemed to regain himself and he started running.

"AAAAAUGH! AAAAAAAAA(etc.)"

He ran like heck, forgetting the stalactites and stalagmites again but thankfully he didn't hit anything. He ran until he heard something stepping faintly ahead... and he stopped dead. It was a horse's hooves on the limestone. It was walking hesitantly in his direction.

He was frozen. He didn't talk. What if it was the evil gray horse...?

He couldn't see the horse, but he knew it was coming. He could hear it breathing, but it sounded nervous and that puzzled him... but the only other horse in the cave was Cloudberry – and he had a hunch that that horse wasn't Cloudberry...

Slowly they moved towards each other, but Drake was

the only one who knew he was going towards someone else. He thought he might bravely face the evil horse.

The horse, however, caught a scent of him, but it just kept walking. It probably was just an old scent, meaning someone had come through here earlier.

More hoof steps, more foot steps.

Bump. Drake ran into a horse. But this horse was warm and soft and big… and dark colored… and IT COULD BE A NIGHTMARE–

Bump. The horse ran into the human and stopped dead. He'd never felt a human before… IT WAS NAKED AND TOUCHING HIM–

"AAAAAAAAAAAAAAAAAAAAAAAAAAAAAAA AAAAAAAAAAAAAAAAAAAAAAAAAAAAAAAAA AAAAAAAAAAAAAAAAAAAAAAAAAAAAAAAA AAAAAAAAAA(gasp)AAAAAAAAAAAAAAAAAA AAAAAAAAAAAAAAAAAAAAAAAAAAAAAAAA AAAAAAAAAAAAAAAAAAAAAAAAAAAAAAA AAAAAAAAAAAAAAAAAAUUUUUUGHHHHHHHHH!"

"NEEEEEEEEEEEEEEEEEEEEEEEEEEEEEEEE EEEEEEEEEEEEEEEEEEEEEEEEEEEEEEEEEEEE EEEEEEEEEEEEEEEEEEIIIIIIIIIIIIIIIIIIIIIIIIIIIIIIIIIIIIII IIIIIIIIIIIIIIIIIIIIIIIIIIIIIIIIIIIIIIIIIIIIIIIIIIIIIIIIIIIIIG GGGGGGGGGGGGGGGGGGGGGGGGGGGGGGGGGGGGGG

GGGGGGGGGGGGGGGGGGGGGGGGGGGGGGGHHHHHHH
HHHHHHHHHHHHHHHHHHHHHHHHHHHHHHHHHHHHH
HHHHHHHHHHHHHHHHHHHHHHHHH!"

They screamed very, very loudly. The horse turned, bucked very close to Drake, and ran like heck back the way he came. Drake turned and started to run like heck back to where he had been but he decided the gray horse was still there and he turned around and ran after the horse he had run into instead.

The horse heard the human screaming behind him and ran as fast as he could, neighing in fright. Then there was daylight, and they both came charging out of the cave, Drake many feet behind the horse. They were both blinded by the sudden sunlight, but Drake could see a black horse-with a perfectly normal and non-darkness mane and tail and regular eyes – running for its life into the trees.

Drake kept running. He wanted to be AWAY FROM THE CAVE. He ran screaming until he nearly collided with Nellie.

"NELLIEEEEEEEEEEEEEEEEEEEEEEEEEEEEEE!"

"Drake – what happened to your shirt?!"

"I SAW AN EVIL GRAY HORSE AND RAN INTO A NIGHTMARE, I think, AND I RIPPED MY SHIRT ON A STALACTITE AND... hey! It was YOUR fault!" Drake looked at her terrified-ed-ly and furiously.

Nellie gulped.

A Nightmare? Thought Cloudberry, who was standing near Nellie. *That didn't sound like a Nightmare...* Nightmares had a very high, screechy voice. That voice had almost sound-ed familiar to her... uh oh.

"Drake, what color was the horse? And what color were the horse's eyes?" Cloudberry asked.

"Uhhh... it was a black horse. I don't really know about the eyes, but they weren't red. Hey... you betrayed me!" He put his arms out to gesture the drama of it all. "I could have DIED in there! Those stalactites and stalagmites were EVIL I tell you! None of them hit you guys! And that gray horse nearly scared the (Drake said a word that would have made little kids go 'ooooooooooooooooh you said a baaaaaad wooooooord' in an annoying upwards tone) out of me!"

"Cave horses?" Cloudberry said. She knew of the gray horses with the black eyes. "They are not bad. They are shy. They will come and lead you through the caves."

"Have you met one?"

"Yes. They are invisible – unless they choose not to be."

"Well that would have been nice for me to know when I was running like crazy in danger of killing myself on a cave formation."

He glared at Nellie and complained some more only to have her burst out laughing in his face. He cussed and threatened, but he would never really do anything to her, so instead he stomped over to the edge of the cliff in curiosity.

Nellie followed. Cloudberry didn't come over, instead she went towards the cave. She spied the opening and went to it. The smell of Drake was in her nostrils... and fear... and Nightcloud? She sniffed the side of the cave and sniffed all around until she found some droppings nearby. They were definitely Nightcloud's. He had pooped here not long ago! But it was more like an hour or two ago, not minutes.

Dumb stallions, always have to poop everywhere they go... she thought.

She shuddered and looked around as if he would be there. She must be careful now if he was around. He would surely try to fight her or hurt her... though he would probably be delayed for a day or two because of the scary cave incident. He would fly over the caves now... if he had wings. Unicorn's wings usually were fully grown by the time they were yearlings, but sometimes if the horse got injured it took much longer. Nightcloud had not flown after Cloudberry the last time she had escaped him. He only reared angrily and stomped at her escaping. Surely he would have flown if he could.

Cloudberry returned to where Drake and Nellie were and nickered. They were glaring madly at each other. Cloudberry nuzzled at Drake's arm, and looked down at the peculiar luminous face of his watch. The time said said 4:23, but of course, she didn't know how to tell.

Drake looked at her as she continued to lip at his watch. "Is it time to go? Oh." How will we get down from here?"

Drake did not feel like walking all the way down and around, and he certainly wasn't going in the caves again. Cloudberry said she could fly them both down if they did it one at a time.

Nellie jumped on Cloudberry and they glided down to where the entrance of the cave was. Then she flew back up, and soon Drake was there beside her. He was not quite as angry now but still grumpy.

As they walked away from the cave Drake looked back. In the darkness of the cave's mouth, faintly outlined, was a gray horse. It disappeared into the air when they made eye contact.

"That's what I saw," Drake said later on, pointing to the page with the gray horse on it. They had the book Unicorn Breeds of Uni out again.

Drake looked at his hand that still had faint gray powder on it. He shook it.

Cave unicorn type C

Height: rarely recorded; 12.2 to 15 hands
Temperament: very shy, varies
Color: gray, ranging from pale to dark dapple
Horn type: no horn
Wing type: no wings

This type of cave unicorn is very secretive and shy, and therefore not much is known about them. They are seen in the same area as mirror stone, and if one looks into one of the stones then the invisible creatures become visible. They do not make noise and they dwell inside caves, making themselves invisible if an intruder comes. However, if the adventurer somehow becomes lost, the horses will lead them out by appearing and disappearing, until the adventurer has found the way out of the cave. This leads to the belief that they are good-natured, though their black, pupil-less eyes seem less than friendly. If a person or other creature looks into a mirror stone and sees one, and reaches out to touch it, they will not feel the equine there, but there will be a bit of gray powder on the hand. This is a mystery to many but the powder is not toxic and washes off easily with water. What they eat is unknown, but they may lick water off of the sides of the wetter caves and eat mushrooms, as guessed by scientists.

"They're so weird looking," said Nellie.

"Yeah, and they have bad eyesight," Drake said, reading some more. "But I'd expect so, living in the dark all their lives."

"They can *see* in the dark," Cloudberry said. "That's why they don't go running into you and getting you covered with gray powder."

"Speaking of gray powder…"

Valerie walked up behind him. She had found Nellie's account of what had happened very, very hilarious. "Here's a shirt, you wimp," she said. She gave him a green shirt with *cute but psycho* on it. Underneath it was Happy Bunny. How was Happy Bunny in Uni? The world may never know.

"What! I refuse to wear this girly shirt!"

"Okay. Then go around all day showing off your six pack." She rolled her eyes and walked off.

Drake poked at his flat, soft belly. He really wasn't that wimpy was he?

"Drake I think you'd definitely better wear that so you don't get cold. Besides it fits you well. You're more girly looking than I am." She snickered.

Drake cussed and put that shirt on. He needed to work out or something.

Nellie was still flipping through the book. She came to

a picture of a handsome black Arabian. She wanted a horse like that!

There were many kinds of unicorns named after the earth versions. Thoroughbreds, Quarter Unicorns, Arabians of course, Mustang, even gaited Staperville Walking Unicorns. She guessed Staperville was a place. Odd name.

Nellie wondered why they would bother to have a "walking" unicorn breed since they could talk, couldn't anyone teach their horse how to do a special gait? She could teach Cloudberry how to pace easily.

They soon ate dinner and learned that the next day Lorelei and Valerie would be gone in the morning. They were going to go have breakfast with their friends, DRAGONS, who had invited them in as thanks for trying to fix Zenny.

"Zenny came over and said that they would have cloud berries and waffles for breakfast." Lorelei said. "It sounds too good to pass up. He's going to come over tomorrow and we'll ride him to his house."

"What about me?" Alidar protested. "There is no way I'm going to a dragon's house! I'll get salmonella or something like that!!"

"We'll bring you back some stuff, then," Valerie said.

Alidar got all pouty. "What'll I do tomorrow morning when I'm all alone?"

"I can ride you," said Nellie hopefully. "Drake's going to leave me alone and go ride Cloudberry but we could follow him."

He looked at her. "Well, okay..." Alidar said with un-Alidar-ish-ness.

The next morning Nellie's watch woke her up at 9:00 and, of course, Drake was already up and gone. Alidar was dozing near her, waiting, and she soon jumped on him and they started following where she guessed they had gone.

"When did everyone leave?" Nellie asked Alidar in annoyance.

"Well Zenny came at eight and tried to get me to come, but I don't trust him so I came over here. And Drake and Cloudberry left ten minutes ago, I think, because they were there when I was falling asleep."

"That dirtbag!" said Nellie of Drake. "He knew I wanted to go with him."

Soon they saw a familiar white unicorn up ahead and they snuck up behind her. Nellie had a big stick that she had picked up earlier and she poked the rider with it. He lost his balance and fell.

"AAGHK-" Drake said in confusion, falling. He fell smack on the ground for the millionth time since he had started riding. He saw Nellie and glared madly. She dropped the stick innocently. "Nellie did you have to follow me?" he grumbled.

"Yes."

Cloudberry was surprised to see them. She didn't mind having company, though. Drake climbed back on her and they started trotting.

"We're going to see that redhead girl again," Drake said.

"Oh. Do you *like* her?" Nellie asked slyly. "Is that why you didn't want me to follow?"

"No!!"

"I don't think your shirt is going to make you any more manly," she said.

Drake grumbled and Cloudberry trotted faster.

Alidar had to trot twice as fast to keep up with Cloudberry's big, smooth strides and Nellie leaned back. It was easier that way. Alidar puffed tiredly and broke into a canter. Thankfully his canter was very smooth and not as tiring and he drew alongside Cloudberry.

They stopped and rested soon. Alidar was all sweaty, shedding, and Nellie was glad she had pants on to keep from getting hairy. They were near the place where the redhead girl's tent was. Drake sat down in the grass.

"I wonder if Valerie and Lorelei are having a good time." Drake said. "Maybe Zenny and his family were secretly evil and wanted to eat them. Maybe we'll never see them again."

"I dunno... I like Zenny. He doesn't seem like he could be evil if he tried." replied Nellie.

"Yeah, but I guess we'll know if we never hear from them again."

Alidar's eyes were gigantic at that idea. Cloudberry nuzzled him reassuringly. "I'm sure the humans are just joking," she said.

They heard, "Hey you guys!"

They all turned to see an unsurprising sight. The redhead was leading Songoffire towards them. Songoffire had her bridle and reins on, but there was no saddle. "I just got done riding."

She removed Songoffire's reddish-brown leather bridle. It had some rhinestones in the brow band that made it look fancy.

"Hey. I came to ask you some stuff... if you would erm... have some advice..." Drake said, stepping forward. "I want to be a jockey... and I need to get a license."

She tossed her silky hair. "Well, I see you have a unicorn. And you are fifteen aren't you? There you go."

"But wait, what about the parents? Don't I need parents there?"

"Ahh, it doesn't matter. As long as you look 15 and have a fast horse they'll give you a license. At least that's the way it was at the track I went to."

"Well that seems easy," Drake said.

"They had a special challenge when I went there, and if you beat their fastest time for galloping a half mile then you can get a license free. That's how I got mine."

"Cool! Then I guess I'm off to get a license... wait. I have no saddle or bridle or anything."

"Well then you'll have to save money until you can buy one... and I'd recommend a used one. It doesn't have to be racing, but I don't think they want you riding bareback and bridleless, even if you do have a good unicorn."

Drake groaned. He must get money...

"I've seen this filly running around before," the redhead said, pointing to Cloudberry. "She's pretty fast, though not as fast as Songoffire... you might be able to win some distance races with her."

"We'll win more than that," Drake said confidently.

"What about you?" The redhead asked Nellie.

"Oh this isn't my unicorn…" Nellie said quickly. "I don't have one. But I will as soon as I find a nice one. Maybe a black one."

"Why a black one? Well okay, whatever…" she turned to Drake. "Hey, Drake it is, right? Do you want to race?"

She was challenging him. "Yeah!" he said. He ran over to Cloudberry and tried to climb up her mane, but he went too fast and accidentally made her sink to the left and he fell. He got up and brushed himself off, embarrassed. He managed to get up there the second time.

"Alright, miss……uhhmm… what is your name?"

"I'm Blaise… Blaise Cooper." She said it as if she was the most famous person in the world.

Woah… Drake thought. "Oh. Okay we're ready to race!" Cloudberry bounced and half-reared eagerly. "Whoa!" Drake said, glad he had been holding the mane.

"We'll race around that tree and back," Blaise said, pointing to a small tree that was a good 50 feet away from the tightly woven trees of the forest. "Your sister can be the finish line."

The tree was a long way away from them. Drake gulped. But Cloudberry was confident. She could go to that tree and back, it wasn't more than a third of a mile away.

Blaise called Songoffire and she came and obediently

stuck her head in the bridle that Blaise was still holding. Blaise jumped up onto her bare back, and they lined up.

"Do you know what to do, Cloudberry?" Drake asked nervously. Cloudberry bobbed her head.

"Hold on to my mane," she said.

Nellie waited until they were both still.

"On your mark... get set..."

Songoffire tossed her head in impatience.

"Go!"

Cloudberry was ready this time, and went flying forward, but Songoffire was quicker and out sprinted her. Cloudberry's strides were big, but her legs were going slow. She sped up. Soon she was really running. Surprisingly quickly, she passed Songoffire, who seemed to have slowed. Maybe she had burnt out already. But they weren't even to the tree!

Her hooves pounded on the grass, making thudding sounds, even though she seemed not to touch the earth. She galloped high above the ground, Drake holding on to her mane and leaning forward. They could hear Songoffire behind them, with her quick, rapid hoof beats. They were getting very near to the tree.

Cloudberry slowed, not sure of how she could go about such a sharp turn, and Songoffire passed her, shortened her strides, lifted her shoulders, and skidded right around it. Blaise seemed to be one with her, staying with her every movement. Cloudberry took the turn much wider. Coming out straight again, she ran furiously after the red mare, catching her.

Nellie could see them coming fast. "GO DRAKE! GO CLOUDBERRY!" she hollered, laughing. She wasn't exactly the cheerleader type, but she hopped up and down. Alidar looked at her strangely.

Cloudberry was starting to get tired, but she managed to pass Songoffire. Songoffire was still going at a surprisingly lower pace. Cloudberry had slowed some because of the tiring, but she knew she would win. She had to. Songoffire wasn't nearly as fast as she looked.

They were coming up on Nellie quickly. Cloudberry raised her head, then suddenly, the hoof beats behind them blurred into a frightening sounding run, and in an instant, Songoffire went flying past her! She started to speed up after her, but she saw they were too close to the finish and Songoffire won by a length, going away!

Cloudberry slowed down gradually, curving around and stopping at Nellie. Songoffire and Blaise were there. Songoffire was puffing. She didn't arch her neck or show off. She seemed to act like it was nothing to even be proud of.

157

"Well, like I said, just not fast enough," said Blaise cockily.

"Ahh, we could have caught you if there was more room," Drake said. He looked sideways.

"But I'm afraid it's the quickest horse who gets the prize," said Blaise. She grinned a million dollar grin. "You guys could sure get a jockey license, but you'd be better off staying out of sprints and big races."

And with that, she and her horse pranced off to walk. Drake and Cloudberry lipped, mocking her.

"Gosh she's hot though…" Drake said after a moment. Cloudberry shrugged him off sideways.

"Come on, we need to go back to the house to see if Valerie and Lorelei are there," said Alidar worriedly. "This race was enough exercise for Cloudberry, don't you think?"

"It's 10:02, Drake said. "I think that 10:30 is when they said they'd be back the very earliest."

Alidar grumbled as Nellie mounted him and they started walking.

Cloudberry was hot and a little tired, more from the excitement than the running. They walked for a long time, through the woods in the shade.

"Let's run, Alidar," Nellie said while Drake and Cloudberry were walking. Alidar started to canter, and she squeezed his sides, urging him. He grunted in annoyance and started running, though he didn't like running very much. It was only the ones who loved to run, Nellie thought, that won races.

Nellie leaned back when they were getting further away, and he shortened his small strides and slowed down to trot finally. Trotting was his favorite speed. And Nellie didn't mind his nice smooth ride, so they trotted around for a while.

"Alidar, was your mother a Paso Fino?" she asked teasingly.

"One of those little prissy things?" he asked. If a Paso Fino unicorn had been around, it probably would have kicked his butt. "Of course not! My mother was an Arab unicorn. She still runs wild with Sunridge's herd."

"Which is she? Nellie asked.

"The flea bitten gray," he said simply.

"Nellie... nnneeeelllllllliiieeee..." they heard.

"I think Drake is calling us," said Nellie. "Maybe Valerie and Lorelei came back. Let's go."

Alidar ran like the wind! But Drake was still just walking around when they found him again.

He looked at Nellie. "I found a cool thing," he said. He pointed to a tree with a large knothole in it. "Look, and I promise you it's not a portal!"

Nellie hopped off of Alidar, came over and looked in. She couldn't see it, so she put her head all the way in.

"CHI CHIIIIIIIIIIIIIIIIIIIIII!"

The creature inside screeched and attacked her hair madly from above. Drake almost fell down, laughing uncontrollably, but Nellie didn't notice, pulled her head out quick as a buttery Alidar, and ran around screaming with the thing on her head.

"AAAAAAAAAAAAGH GET IT OFF GET IT OFFGETITOFFGETITOFFGETITOFF!!"

The squirrel-like creature (it was green) jumped off of her head as she passed the tree again and landed on a limb. Nellie stopped freaking out eventually and saw it.

"Oh, hey you're just a little squirrley! You meant me no harm!"

The squirrel thingy flicked her off.

"WHY YOU SON OF A…"

"No Nellie! That's how they say hello!" Alidar warned her before she tried to choke the poor thing to death.

"Oh. Sorry!"

She looked at it disapprovingly. It eyed her warily and crawled off into its hole.

"HAHAHAHA(etc.)" laughed Drake.

Nellie came over and punched him. Then she smoothed her hair out and jumped on Alidar and they walked off.

Man, every time I try to get revenge she punches me. Sisters are no fun. Thought Drake unhappily, lying on the ground clutching his stomach. Cloudberry nuzzled him.

Alidar and Nellie went back to the house. Lorelei and Valerie still weren't home yet. Nellie could see the house clock in the window. It was 10:47... time went by so fast while riding. Why couldn't it be like that at school?

But, Nellie thought, she didn't have to go to school anymore! She lived here now... even if Lorelei would let them use the portal to get back, she didn't think she'd go but to visit. Life was so bland back there... but here it was so calm and happy. She knew what she was going to do, she'd be a jockey... she used to not know what she would be. It kept her awake at night.

She would rather be a dumb jockey who never finished school than a smart office worker, stuck sitting in the air conditioning and lights all day. She was sure that Drake would agree.

As soon as they could win races and get rich they could

build a house here, and there would be stables and they would breed Cloudberry after they retired her (providing she WANTED to be bred) and have little foals running around, and they could train them and win some more races with them. And, no offense to Drake, but her black horse would be faster than Cloudberry and they would kick his butt in races, though Cloudberry would still be a fast racehorse.

Nellie slid off of Alidar. The buckskin colt/stallion looked worriedly out onto the plains. Where were Lorelei and Valerie? Had they really been eaten? What if they had?

Alidar was aware of a little buzzing sound and Noopie came floating towards him, out of the open window of the house. He had been left behind because Lorelei feared he would be inhaled by a dragon or some other accidental death like that.

"Noopie, they're not back yet and I think they might have been... eaten by the dragons!"

Noopie squeaked in horror.

"Really! What if we never see them again... I hope they come back soon! Zenny wouldn't eat them, would he?"

Nellie listened to them freaking out, but instead of trying to calm the uncalmable she went over to the clearing they lived in now. Their little shelter was still there in the woods, but Sunridge had probably pooped all over it or eaten it or something… dumb stallions.

She picked up the Uni breeds book and looked through it. Miniature unicorn, arctic unicorn, the sky horse…

Presently, she heard someone crying and she looked up. Alidar… she didn't know unicorns cried. She walked over to where Noopie and Alidar were freaking out. It was 11:08.

"What on earth is wrong?"

"Lorelei and Valerie still haven't come back," Alidar said tearfully. "I think they-"

"They did NOT get eaten! Gosh! That's just Drake being retarded!"

She drew Alidar's head to her chest and tried to calm him like she always did with her younger siblings.

"You are so worrisome," she said. "No wonder everyone says Arabians are high strung."

Very soon Nellie heard thumping and Zenny came galloping (well sort of…) over the hill with Lorelei and Valerie.

Alidar neighed and left Nellie and ran to them. They jumped off of Zenny and thanked him and he left.

"What's wrong?" Valerie asked Alidar as he skidded to a stop in front of her and nuzzled her, his eyes gigantic with tears.

"Valerie! I thought you got eaten!!"

"Huh?" Valerie looked past him at Nellie. "Nellie… have you been telling him things?!"

"No, Drake did." Nellie sighed.

"Drake said that if you guys weren't back by 11 then you got eaten by dragons and I'll have no owner and have to be a wild unicorn with no friends-"

"The dragons were perfectly nice, Alidar. They did not try to eat us! They gave us waffles! It just took a long time to eat them!"

"What's going on? They didn't get eaten?" Drake was back from his ride. He came up, saying that.

Valerie punched him.

Ahh my spleen, thought Drake, lying on the ground once more.

Chapter 7

When tack attacks

"Valerie, I'm going to need to use that saddle you said you had. I want to start racing Cloudberry soon," Drake said that night at the dinner table. He had recovered from being punched and was now thinking about racing. He knew he could become a jockey now so the sooner the better.

"Are you sure? It's a small saddle. The girth might not fit. Though… Alidar is pretty wide for a little horse..." Valerie tapped her chin.

Alidar had been staying near Valerie the whole rest of the day, still paranoid about the dragon thing.

"Do you mean to say I'm fat?" He commented, his ears going back and forward.

"No." Valerie looked away innocently. "What about a bridle? The bridle I have is pretty small too." She told Drake.

"Cloudberry has a small head."

"I'll show you the stuff tomorrow morning. But the chances are Cloudberry might not like you anymore if you put a saddle on her..." she eyed him.

"No, I told her about it. And she says that if she's racing she won't notice. Besides... we're buds! Why do we have to wait until tomorrow?"

"I was hoping you'd die of suspense or something," she said sarcastically.

"What does the saddle look like?" Drake asked, trying to get more information.

"Well, it's an English saddle. 15 ½ inch, all purpose with knee rolls, not sure of the brand. Havana colored."

"Huh?"

"Ahh, Drake. I must teach you more."

"Well, here's the stuff," Valerie said the next day, as she opened a wooden door. Her lip wrinkled. "Eww... I think I'd better get you some rags and oil."

"Where is it?" Drake asked eagerly. The only thing in the closet/tack room on the side of Alidar's stall was a box of brushes and a big lump of green moldy stuff.

"There's the saddle. I haven't oiled it or cleaned it or anything in a long time."

She pointed to the lump of mold. Drake groaned. "And I think the bridle's down there somewhere on the floor."

She left to go get Drake some rags and oil, and Cloudberry came over to see the saddle. Drake was trying to pick it up with a big stick. He got it out but it fell as he turned and green powder and a few bugs flew all around. Cloudberry shied madly and they both ran.

Soon the dust settled and the bugs flew away and they went back over to the saddle. "I'm glad the mold blows off," said Drake. "I didn't know saddles did that. Hey, that gives me an idea…"

He went inside and asked, "Lorelei, have you got a leaf blower I can use?" She didn't have one, but she definitely knew what one was. She did a magical leaf blower spell, and one appeared.

"Don't tell Lorelei I did that. It's illegal." she said. Drake laughed madly and ran outside with the leaf blower ready.

"Watch out, Valerie, I'll get the first layer off! EXTREME SADDLE CLEANING!!"

He turned the leaf blower on and it blew madly at the saddle. And, of course, a huge cloud of dust and mold arose. Everyone backed up.

Soon the big cloud of dust was too big and Drake gave it some time to settle. Then he turned the saddle over and attacked it again on the other side. Extreme saddle cleaning was fun!

Eventually, nothing more would blow off the saddle, so Drake picked it up and carried it away from the dust/mold covered area and he and Valerie started wiping it with the rags. Cloudberry watched curiously.

Soon they had it oiled and un-moldy and as good as new. Valerie didn't hesitate to say she hoped the stirrup leathers wouldn't break.

"Now for the bridle," said Drake.

He found the bridle lying on the floor surrounded by a few mushrooms. He made a face and dropped it on the ground and commenced to blowing the mold off of it. Then they oiled it.

"This needs a new bit," Valerie said. The bit was rusty and had a hard coat of mold on it. "I think it used to be a D-ring snaffle, but I'm not sure now..."

The bridle had rainbow colored reins, and Drake noticed they appeared to be made out of an old jump rope.

"Well it was there, so I used it," Valerie said as he looked at her. "I'm going to go ask Lorelei if she'll conjure up a bit for us."

"Why can't you do it? I though you were magical. You made the leaf blower appear. Is their something about bits...?"

"Shut uuuup!"

"Gosh."

Drake followed her. "Lorelei! We need a new bit for Cloudberry," Valerie said.

"What kind?" Lorelei said as she looked out the door."

"The most non – harsh kind you can think of," Drake said.

Lorelei said some magic words mixed with 'soft bit', and a bit appeared in her hand magically. It was a loose ring snaffle bit, and it appeared to be covered with a light colored rubber on each side. It was English style, with the reins also attached to the sides.

"I know you needed some new reins, too," she said.

"Hey why can't you just make a brand new saddle appear?" Drake asked.

"Too big and expensive. It would take a lot of magicalness that I need for other stuff. Besides, it would be too easy for you."

Drake grumbled and walked out. They attached the bit to the bridle, and Valerie adjusted the sides so it was the biggest it could be. It looked pretty good, they thought.

"Let's see if it fits," Drake said.

Cloudberry eyed the bridle, but the bit smelled like an apple so she let them put it in her mouth, and then they eased the headstall on (it had a special extra buckle to get the horn through). They buckled the throatlatch loosely.

Cloudberry played with the bit and tossed her head, seeing if the bridle would fly off, but no such luck.

"It fits pretty well," Valerie said.

"Id asds lig abble," Cloudberry said, unable to move her tongue enough to say it properly. (It tastes like apple!)

"It looks good. Like a racehorse." Drake said admiringly, winking at Cloudberry.

"Then let's see if the saddle fits."

Valerie took the saddle and put it on Cloudberry's back. She was a little taller than Drake, so she could see it better.

"Don't we need a pad?" Drake asked.

"Not for seeing if it fits. I have a pad in the shed too, but I think it needs to be washed."

Valerie pulled the girth under and tightened it as loose as it would go. Cloudberry's head shot up with the unfamiliar squeezing.

"I WON' EE A'LE TO EATHE!" she protested. (I WON'T BE ABLE TO BREATHE!)

"Yes, you will. You'd be surprised," said Alidar, who had been watching for a minute.

The saddle wasn't on very tight, but it was tight enough,

and Cloudberry's skin twitched and she swished her tail. She gave Drake a look.

"Remember, you said you'd forget it when you ran," Drake said. "You'll get used to it and it won't matter. Just be glad I'm not putting some big heavy western saddle on you!" That could come later. After all, who said that just because Drake wanted to be a jockey, he wasn't a wannabe cowboy?

They soon took the saddle and the bridle off. Cloudberry drooled and licked her lips for the next few minutes as the taste and feel of the bit lingered. Valerie went back to the tack closet and got another green thing out. Drake groaned. Something they hadn't seen?

"Relax, it's a saddle pad," Valerie said. Drake saw thankfully that it had barely any mold on it and its color was bright light green. It matched the green reins that Lorelei had put on the bridle.

"It's dirty and damp," Valerie said. "I'll wash it tonight." They heard the house door shut, and footsteps.

"Hey, is this the new saddle?" Nellie said, coming over.

"Where have you been?" Drake asked.

"I was inside watching TV. There was a horse cartoon on. It was awesome."

Drake rolled his eyes.

"Why is everything so dusty? And why is there a leaf blower over there?"

"EXTREME saddle cleaning!" Drake said.

Nellie raised one eyebrow. "Does the stuff fit Cloudberry?"

"The saddle doesn't seem to pinch her, and the bridle fits fine," said Valerie. "It'll work well enough."

"Well… I haven't ridden Cloudberry yet today, so I guess we can go do that," Drake said. "Thanks for letting us use your stuff."

"It's only so you guys will get money to pay us back," said Valerie, trying to seem like she didn't care as much. "And you can use those brushes too because Cloudberry looks like she needs to get the rest of her winter hair out. If you go riding, use the bridle, but wait until I get the pad ready to use the saddle." Valerie waved and walked back to the house.

Drake set the saddle's stand back up, which was lying on the floor of the tack closet, and he put the saddle on it. He left the bridle out to use and he got the brushes.

There was a pretty good selection of brushes. Drake took a currycomb and curried Cloudberry with it, as he had seen the racehorse grooms do. White hair flew off, and Cloudberry lipped happily. This was better than the pinecones!

Nellie watched, standing next to Alidar. Alidar was concentrating on Cloudberry.

She poked his shoulder teasingly.

"Do you like her?"

"What? No! No I do not!" he screeched.

Drake and Cloudberry looked at him strangely wondering what he was screeching about. Nellie could almost feel the heat radiating from him. He definitely liked her.

"You lie," she said.

Alidar was glad they were too far away to hear. "Well… what unicorn doesn't?"

Nellie put her hand on his muzzle. His whiskers were long. He was warm.

"Are you Lorelei's unicorn, or are you Valerie's?" she asked suddenly.

"Valerie's. Lorelei used to own me but she's always busy and Valerie is the only one who rides me."

"I rode you!"

"Yeah… but you're annoying!"

Nellie humphed and turned away from him.

Drake was now smoothing Cloudberry's coat with the soft brush. She had no dirt on her at all.

"Don't you ever get dirty?" he asked.

"Yes, of course, but then I just wash it off in a stream or rain."

"Oh." Drake took a hairbrush out of the box, picked a few ancient black hairs out of it, and started to comb her silky mane. The brush went through it like a liquid. Drake went over to the other side, and he flopped the sections of mane that had fallen on that side over. It looked a little better when all the hair was on the left side.

"Okay, Cloudberry, I'm going to clean the underside of your hooves," he said since none of her hair needed more brushing.

"What?"

"You just pick your hoof up and don't fall on me." Drake got a hoof pick out of the box and leaned on Cloudberry. She picked her hoof up and he took it. Cloudberry leaned on him.

"Cloudberry... I am not... your... leg..." Drake said, getting squashed.

Cloudberry shifted her weight onto her other three legs.

Her hooves were hard and flat. They were worn down, too. Drake wondered how they got worn down if the horse lived in the clouds, because didn't they need some rough rock or dirt or something?

He did all of her hooves, which didn't really need cleaning, and brushed off the dirt. He finished quickly. He petted her muzzle and his hand went up to her forehead, and he touched her silvery white horn.

He's touching my horn! He heard ring through his mind.

WHOA! Thought Drake. *I can hear her thoughts this way!*

You can? He heard again.

Cloudberry?

What? Huh?

Hi! Thought Drake.

You're weird, thought Cloudberry.

We can speak telepathically! This rocksssssss.

Well, now that Drake had learned this cool information, he decided Cloudberry was groomed enough and he went and got her bridle off of the ground again.

She raised her muzzle and curled her upper lip at him.

"Well, okay then, if you don't want to take it then you'll never be allowed to race and I'll have to find another unicorn."

Cloudberry lowered her head reluctantly. She liked having Drake as a friend, even if he was kind of annoying at points. Drake slipped her bridle on, being careful not to let the bit hit her teeth, and patted her.

Suddenly Cloudberry grunted, and she sunk down onto her knees.

"What's wrong!?"

"I'm trying to make it easier for you to get on! What does it look like I'm doing?"

Drake looked at her, surprised. "Well thank you, Cloudberry." He got on her and she rose up again.

"Show off," Nellie heard Alidar mutter.

Cloudberry trotted off into the woods, Drake sitting her trot easily. He kept the reins very loose. Cloudberry would turn if he pointed in a direction. He sat up straight and looked ahead of him like an Indian.

"If I pull the left rein then you must go left, and if I pull the right you must go right. If I pull back which I probably won't often do then it means to stop. Racehorses can lean on the bit for balance, since they are so tilted forward when they run, so you need to get used to it." He tried to sound professional, even though he knew he wasn't. Drake hoped he had at least a few things right.

He pulled the right rein gently and turned his upper

body. Cloudberry turned slightly, listening more to his position than the rein.

Cloudberry had a soft, tender mouth and if Drake pulled she drew her head back like a fancy dressage horse. He did not want to hurt her so he dropped the reins eventually and just held the mane. Cloudberry liked that much more.

"Hey Drake... do you want to fly?" She asked later as they were walking around. "Up in the clouds?"

If Drake was a horse, his ears would have perked, but in nervousness as much as excitement.

"Really? I don't know... I've never flown very high before... maybe I need a saddle..."

"I can't flap my wings out with one of those on. And... and don't you want to see the cloud unicorns? My mother's up there, along with lots of cloud berries that are better than chocolate."

"I really want to. Erm... but what if I fall?" Drake was brave to an extent, but still fearful of being so high on a horse when he barely knew how to ride.

"I'll catch you!"

"Hey wait, I have an idea," said Drake. He told her.

They went back to Lorelei's house. Drake found a rope, and he tied the end into a loop and slipped it over Cloudberry's neck. He had some trouble with the horn but he managed to get it over. It was not too tight, but it would not slip off easily either. He knotted it so it was in a firm loop that wouldn't expand or tighten.

He tied the other end around his waist in his belt loops. There, now if he fell he wouldn't go all the way down... he ulped at the thought.

"Okay, let's go!" said Cloudberry, twitching her skin at the rope's feeling.

"Wait one minute," said Drake. He undid the horn strap and the throat latch of the bridle and slipped it off. "You've figured the bridle out enough."

Drake got on her and he held the rope as she warned him to sit on her rump. He did and she flapped her wings out magically with little sparkles and things flying around like in the movies.

She started to trot out into the open, past Sunridge's territory, where they never dared to go. Drake stayed ahead of her wings and leaned forward, holding her mane. They beat on either side of him oddly as Cloudberry cantered, getting ready to lift off.

She jumped into the air and started to fly upwards. It was like she was rearing, and Drake felt himself slipping back. If he fell off, he might accidentally choke Cloudberry, seeing as how the rope was on her neck... why hadn't he thought of that before? Even if it slid down around her chest and shoulders like he thought...

The white filly felt him sliding back, and leveled out some, making her ascent less hurried. Drake got a better bunch of her mane and wrapped his hands in it. They were flying... him and his unicorn friend?

He looked down and gasped. They were very high now... he could see the top of the forest like a map. There was the house and there was a dot, which was a person, but he couldn't tell who. There was another dot on the other side of the forest, probably Blaise.

The clouds were getting closer. This was like when he had flown Alidar, only they were going higher... the earth below them was green, but over in the distance, there was a morning blue-green sea.

"There are mountains far that way," Cloudberry said pointing her nose to the East. Drake could hardly see them, faint outlines on the green horizon. Drake had always liked looking at mountain pictures.... maybe one day him and Cloudberry could go on a mountain ride.

The clouds were very close to them. They passed a low one… a small white cumulus cloud. Drake looked up, and could see the gray shadowed bottoms of the others, outlined in golden sunlight. Drake flattened himself to Cloudberry as they passed directly through part of a cloud… they came out covered in water droplets and cold. Drake gasped as he noticed Cloudberry's sudden faint rainbow colors, but she dried quickly as she flew and they disappeared.

"Your dots came up!"

"Yes. The rain droplets in the clouds make them come."

It's cold..., thought Drake after a moment. *Whoever came up with the idea that clouds were big warm soft pillows?*

Cloudberry began gliding towards a certain cloud. Her cloud. There was a white-skinned unicorn standing on it... it had its ears pricked, and she could tell by the thick neck and arrogance of it that it was a full grown stallion... but it spotted Drake and disappeared into the lumpy white formations of the cloud with a flick of it's tail.

She whinnied, and Drake seemed to know what was next. He braced himself for the landing. They bounced onto the soft cloud and Cloudberry stopped promptly, causing Drake to say oof and fall onto her neck. He saw the whiteness underneath them and squeezed tightly to Cloudberry.

"Will I fall through the cloud since I'm not magical? Is this a cloud unicorn thing?" he asked nervously.

"I don't know... I've never seen a human on one of the clouds before." Cloudberry said sincerely.

Drake had an idea. He took one of his shoes off and dropped it.

The un-magical shoe bounced safely onto the cloud. "I

guess it's ok," Drake said. He slid off of Cloudberry, holding his rope. He didn't fall through. *This feels like a marshmallow,* he thought as he put his shoe back on. It looked like one, too. Rather than water droplets, it was solid.

"I'm going to go in and see if my mom is there," said Cloudberry happily. "You can meet her."

Drake took the rope off of her, and she disappeared around a bulge in the cloud. Drake waited patiently.

In a moment, an older-looking round mare peeked around the side. Her eyes widened, and ears pricked sharply, as if in some sort of amazed terror. Her little foal peeked around too, and quickly hid. Cloudberry, however, pranced out from behind them and went over to Drake.

"This is my, mother," Cloudberry said. "Uhhh... she's named after a cloud too..." (Mammatus, for those of you who have forgotten)

"Hi, mother of Cloudberry," said Drake cheerfully.

The mare pricked one ear and put one back, not sure what to think. Her foal looked again. She shooed it back behind the cloud.

The mare decided to be brave, and she slowly came closer, leaving her foal behind. Her nostrils flared; she came within a few feet and smelled Drake, and she snorted his scent out.

"I'm going to be a racehorse," nickered Cloudberry proudly in horse/unicorn language.

The mare eyed Drake. "He's too happy, I bet he's up to no good." she nickered, and turned around to go back into the cloud.

Cloudberry translated if for Drake. "Dang," said Drake under his breath. Not a good first impression...

They silently followed Cloudberry's mother into the cloud, Drake riding Cloudberry again. The puffy inside of the cloud was colored in pastel natural whites and grays, and sunlight went through the walls, keeping it light. There was a small herd in this cloud. There was a patch of cloud berries growing over by a pool of water-rainwater – which the stallion was drinking out of. He turned to look at the entrance, senses tingling, and saw Drake riding Cloudberry. His eyes got big, and his lower lip lipped in concentration. He wondered if he should bravely fight this intruder or should he burst through the side of the cloud and fly for his life?

Drake jumped off of Cloudberry to pick two cloud berries off the ground that were near. He got back on her, holding them by the stem. They were pinkish colored.

Before the stallion could get P.Oed with them for stealing his berries they turned and left, and the stallion breathed a sigh of relief.

"Hey Cloudberry…" Drake asked half curiously and half nervously as they walked out, "Where do the cloud unicorns go to the bathroom?"

"In hidden places. It's icky, so it just goes through the cloud and sometimes hits some unlucky person below," Cloudberry said. This was the answer that Drake had feared. Now he must always watch out for falling blobs of stinky disgusting and undesirable unicorn poop while he was on the ground.

He got down and picked up the rope and put it on again. He wouldn't fly without it. It was tied securely and tightly around his waist, and he was a little more confident he wouldn't be falling to his death anytime soon.

Cloudberry kneeled on the soft cloud and let Drake get on, and she flapped her wings out and jumped off. They glided through the air. Then Cloudberry began to fly higher, slowly, so Drake increased his death grip on her mane as they went above the clouds. Cumulus clouds are generally the lower clouds where the cloud unicorns live. But Drake and Cloudberry were flying higher into other cloud areas until there were no more clouds around them and they just flew through the air until Drake looked at the sea of white far below them and said that it was probably time to go back down.

Cloudberry glided back down slowly, and Drake relaxed as they passed through the clouds again.

"Hold on real tight," Cloudberry said suddenly."

"Wha-"

Cloudberry's wings stopped flapping. She pointed down and they dive bombed towards the ground.

"AAAGH! WHAT ARE YOU..." but his words were lost in the wind. Drake squeezed Cloudberry and flattened himself to her, trying not to slip back... he could fall off and the rope would tighten and choke her or the rope would break and he'd fall to his doom!

Cloudberry stretched out. She loved to go fast... she dove like that often.

"WHOAAAAAAAA..." Drake screamed, because the ground was getting closer and he worried she might not be able to stop.

Reluctantly, she spread her wings out once again and turned upward, until she was gliding straight again. Drake's legs were around her so tight he was about worse than the saddle! She tolerated him and turned in a large arc. They used the rest of their momentum to glide towards the forest.

Drake had held the cloud berries in his hand with the mane as they flew, and they were still there, just badly blown around.

"You're too cautious to fly with," said Cloudberry. "You're lucky I didn't want to do any back flips or anything."

"THANK you," said Drake, feeling queasy and woozly all over.

Cloudberry landed near the house and cantered back. Alidar and Nellie greeted them.

"So you flew," The buckskin said. He eyed the rope. He looked at Drake, an odd unicorn smile coming onto his features. "I see you didn't trust your riding abilities."

Drake jumped off of Cloudberry and took the rope off. She folded her wings back in, knowing she'd hit them on a tree or something if she left them out.

"What happened to the bridle?" Alidar asked.

"We didn't need it to fly," said Drake.

He took one of the cloud berries and bit into it, the wonderful, better-than-chocolate taste blissful on his taste buds–

"Drake. Did you bring me back a cloud berry?" Nellie had her hands on her hips.

"NO!! NEVER!!" said Drake, hiding behind Cloudberry. "It's MINE!"

Nellie rolled her eyes. Drake gave Cloudberry the other berry, and she must have felt bad so she gave it to Nellie. Nellie split it in half and gave some back to her.

"This is better than cake," said Nellie, munching.

Cloudberry nickered and gave the other half to Alidar. He took it from her, bumped muzzles with her and blushed slightly.

"It's for me? Really? You'd rather me have it than you?"

"I got tired of cloud berries long ago," said Cloudberry. "Grass is better."

Alidar stared at the ground glumly. She wasn't giving up anything she *liked* for him. *Yet again...*

It was late, and Drake's legs were sore from riding. He had never ridden, and then he started doing it for hours at a time... major ouches! He went inside of the house. Nellie followed him. Alidar just stood there, too shy to say anything.

Cloudberry was hungry, of course, so she started grazing. She hadn't gone off alone since Drake had started riding her... maybe tonight she would go and gallop around and fly some more. She'd love to stretch out. But she would come back, of course.

Alidar was staying around and grazed near her. He noticed, out of the corner of his eye, Sunridge peeking out of the woods. He looked sideways at him and pinned his ears, bobbing his nose in the air.

Is the cloud filly Alidar's mare? Thought Sunridge, seeing this. *No way… She belongs to the human, doesn't she? Besides, Alidar is too small… it would never work out!*

Nellie came back out of the house, holding another sort of rope. It was a tape measure. She went up to Cloudberry.

"I'm going to see how many hands tall you are!"

She put the end under her foot and held it up. Nellie could see Cloudberry's withers were at 16.0 hands. Pretty big for a just-turned-three year old.

"No wonder it takes you forever to run fast," said Nellie. "You're so tall and it's all legs."

She measured Alidar just for the heck of it. "14.1,"she said. "Man you're short."

Alidar slunk off.

"No! I didn't mean it that way!"

That night, after dinner, Drake lay down under a tree in the grass. *I hope a bug doesn't crawl in my ear,* he thought as he fell asleep.

Then Nellie came over and brushed her hair, as she always did before bedtime, and scowled at her knotted curls. She laid down under another tree.

Cloudberry was dozing near them, her lip drooping. The pink inside showed. (One would notice that the white skin didn't continue past the exterior.) But she wasn't quite asleep, and as soon as Drake and Nellie were fast asleep she would go for a night run...

The moons brightened the sky. The big one was full. The sky was a dark, dark blue. There were many stars.

Was her father up there?

She would doze for a few more minutes.

Chapter 8

A Midnight Chase,
and the Jockey License

Cloudberry woke with a start. She had heard a noise in the bushes. Sleepily she raised her head. Then she remembered.

Oh, I was going to go running, she thought. She became alert immediately, and walked silently through the trees, not waking Drake or Nellie. She passed the house, passed the sleeping Sunridge, and trotted out into the grassy plains.

The grass brushed her knees as she floated along. But it was only grass, and it swayed with the calm breeze. Suddenly she heard some hoof beats – she stopped and looked.

She could not smell anyone. She was facing the breeze, and scent was downhill. But she saw it, it was a unicorn, too big to be Alidar, and it flitted like a shadow between the trees. Cloudberry was nervous that there was an unknown unicorn there – was it one of Sunridge's herd?

She nervously picked up a canter and thudded through the grass, eager to get away from the unpleasant mystery.

As a gust of wind blew behind her, she sprung into a

gallop, her long strides carrying her high off the ground. Her mane blew back and her tail went up, and she ran for the love of speed – any kind of speed whether it be running or diving through the air and scaring the heck out of Drake. The stars blurred in her vision as she moved like a light through the darkness.

Two dragons lifted their heads as they heard her gallop by. She passed a herd, of which the stallion started to run after her, but she threw grass in his face and left him far behind. She ran past the hill on which the mean redheaded guy lived, but she didn't want to meet him, so she galloped past without looking back.

She ran through the darkness until she could see the far-off lights of a city out there in the middle of the grasslands. That was the way it was in Uni. There were a few random cities of people spread out among the plains. There were also towns, for the less rural people.

She slowed, breathing hard, and gazed at the illuminated dots on the buildings. It was a small city. She hoped it would stay that way. The city goers drove cars instead of riding unicorns or dragons and always wanted to take over more of the land to build on. Their cars and machines smelled bad, and the cloud unicorn's clouds that drifted above the cities never had good water or berries.

Suddenly she heard the flapping of wings. She whirled around and in the darkness she saw a moonlit black unicorn land nearby. It flapped its wings in and stood there.

Cloudberry looked. It had been following her... it flew so it wouldn't make noise. A breeze blew towards her, ruffling the black's shiny mane and tail, and her nostrils quivered with the scent of a colt – but not just any colt. Her own flesh and blood... the only two foals by the gatekeeper, Galaxy Dancer...

"Nightcloud... where have you been?" she nickered in the language of unicorns, which was of course, also the language of horses. The black stallion lifted one foreleg and snorted in a strange way.

"Have you found a herd?" she continued.

"Will a herd ever find me?"

He pawed the ground and snorted again.

"Cloudberry, I could have beaten any stallion to a pulp where I was. But why would I burden myself with mares?" he said icily. "I still must get revenge on you, before I can live."

"Why?"

"I am disgusted with you – you do not understand anything, do you? How thick you are. You have never known what desolation you caused... I almost starved, only to live a pointless life. And you deny it. You deny everything."

Cloudberry never knew what to say when he started this up. Everything only made him madder.

"I didn't know any of that, I was only a foal... and I didn't know you could fly," She said.

"I couldn't fly until months ago... I was injured in the fall because your (Cloudberry's eyes got big at the nasty language!) of a mother abandoned me...remember? She said that father was to come and get me... but they both lied... she wanted me dead."

Cloudberry did not understand. Nightcloud was making no sense to her... but she was ready in case he tried to pull something on her. He repeated this, every time.

"I must get revenge on you... you must know what it feels like to be so close to death." Nightcloud charged.

Cloudberry took off running madly in the direction she came, making Nightcloud do a ninety degree angle turn that slowed him down quite a bit. And yet, with legs flying, he sprinted much faster than her, and she squealed as he raked his teeth on her rump. She kicked at him and hit his breast, though he didn't seem to notice, and he continued running madly after her.

Once she got her strides bigger, she started to pull away, and Nightcloud squealed furiously and turned out such a spurt of speed that he *passed* her. He flung himself into her side, ears pinned flat, making her lose her balance and she nearly fell. She righted herself and came back at him with her head down. She would have stabbed him with her horn right there, because he was mad – but he suddenly stumbled and she galloped past air.

She did not wonder if he was possibly hurt because she heard a scream of rage and more hoof beats – but now she had a big lead on him. She put her head out straight and concentrated on moving her legs faster. Nightcloud was catching her, but she heard his heavy breathing... he was tiring! Cloudberry was tired too, but she took bigger strides than him and was lighter than him. He wasn't catching her so fast now.

She ran and ran until she felt her lungs would burst... but Nightcloud behind her was beaten and he flapped his wings out and rose into the air. He couldn't fly nearly as fast as she could gallop.

"Cloudberry, do not forget I know where you are, always, and I will get revenge on you." He flew upwards, unable to say more because he needed to breathe.

Cloudberry gave a buck of pleasure as she galloped for home. There was a tiny bit of light on the horizon... morning would be soon. She would be safe from Nightcloud if Drake was with her.

"What happened to your butt?" Drake asked the next morning, noticing the bleeding bite. Cloudberry had gone back to sleep and slept until the humans had woken her up. She was tired and sore. So much had happened yesterday.

"Last night..."

"Was it Alidar? Did he turn evil suddenly?"

She shook her head. "I went for a run last night... but I was followed by my brother... and he chased me and tried to hurt me. I outran him."

Nellie listened closely. Her brother was there?

"Your brother?"

"Yes, I have an evil brother. He wants to get revenge on me for some reason."

"What did you do to him to make him want revenge?"

"Nothing. I never did anything. And yet he said I needed to feel what it was like to be near death."

"For no reason at all?" Drake was puzzled.

"That guy sounds insane," said Nellie. *Maybe Sunridge was right when he warned me.*

"I don't know... He wasn't crazy when he was a foal... I

think something happened to him that made him real angry at me and my mom."

"Then why doesn't he go and kick your mom's butt?"

"He thinks he hates her... I think deep down he would never hurt her. And he doesn't want to see her again. It's only me and probably my dad has something to do with it, though I don't know what because he never met him."

"What? What happened to your dad?"

"He's the gatekeeper of the portals and is always in outer space."

"Now that's different," said Drake.

"Well, did your mom do... mean stuff to him?" asked Nellie.

"No... she never did *anything* to him, really... she put her ears back at him whenever he tried to come close to her. And then one day she went over to him and led him away and he looked really happy and that was the last I saw of him until we were older."

"Maybe she neglected him. And took care of you, and that's why he's angry at you." Nellie said. "Out of jealousy."

"Probably." She breathed out through her nostrils softly. "She didn't even tell me he was my brother until after he had gone away."

"That cold hearted..."

"Now hold on! It's not that she doesn't like him. She always asks me about him when I see her."

"Then why did she leave him?"

"Maybe I'll ask my mom that one day," said Cloudberry. "She surely would tell me now that I am almost a mare. And it might help to know, since he probably wants to kill me and all."

"Almost a mare? You only just turned three… right?"

"I have been through three springs," said Cloudberry.

"You're not a mare yet, then."

"For a wild horse I would be called a mare."

Soon they decided to stop talking about Cloudberry's brother, and promised to keep an eye out for him. He could come any time and threaten them.

Cloudberry was very tired so Drake decided not to ride her. She stood sleeping under a tree with one hind leg cocked. She would have lied down, to rest her legs, but she was still a bit jumpy.

She woke and followed Drake when he went to Lorelei's house. He went inside and she felt content standing outside the front porch dozing.

She heard a hoof crush a twig behind her and jumped. She kicked out, and Alidar jumped to the side, surprised.

"Oh, Alidar. It's you. Sorry."

Alidar just eyed her and walked past, his ears in the okay-you're-freaked-out-and-I'm-going-over-there position.

But then, Alidar thought, he would only be missing a chance to be a manly stallion around Cloudberry. So he went back over to her.

"What's wrong?" he asked, his gentle green eyes looking over her face.

"Nothing. Nothing at all."

"Okay" and Alidar walked away. *Oh, good job being a manly horse,* he thought to himself sarcastically, frowning.

While Drake ate breakfast he started writing a letter. It was to his mom. He didn't know how long he had been in Uni, exactly, but he guessed maybe a week and a half.

> Dear mom,
> I hope you haven't called the detectives or anything to find me and Nellie because we are doing fine and we live in the land of unicorns and

Drake stopped there and crumpled up the paper. That

was crappy... he had never been good at writing. He started over:

> Dear mom,
> I know this may sound scary but I'm not going to be coming home for some time, I think. Nellie and I are doing fine. We live in a new place, and there are horses here and I have one and I'm going to get a jockey license and race it because it's fast. Don't look for me on TV, because I won't be there. Don't look for me with police or anything, because it will only be a waste of money. I say that because we are so happy where we are. We are going to build a house as soon as I get rich from racing and then I'll send money home. It will show we are doing well.
>
> Drake

He drew a picture of a horse on the envelope, and its head was too big and it looked like a deranged My Little Pony. But Drake's mom knew how he drew horses, and she would know it was he that had drawn it and not someone else.

"All right, I guess I'm ready to mail this."

Lorelei called Alidar and she pulled her wand. "Alidar, can you take Drake's letter to his mom?"

"I guess."

"I'm going to turn you into a bird. And you fly to the portal and when you get to earth find the address," Lorelei said. She said a few funky sorceress-y words and Alidar turned into a pigeon.

"Couldn't you have turned me into something more dignified?" he squawked.

Lorelei agreed that that breed of bird made him look fat, so she turned him into a raven. She showed him the address and he took the folded letter in his claw, and he flew -a little awkwardly – off into the forest. Drake wished he could follow to see where that portal was.

"I wonder if mom is worried or relieved that we're gone?" wondered Nellie aloud.

Suddenly they heard a neigh of fright from outside. Cloudberry was rearing.

Everyone ran out so see what was happening. But, it turned out, there was only a blue roan stallion outside covered in bumps. He was scratching himself madly on the house. *Probably came to see Lorelei,* thought Drake.

Cloudberry was relieved that it was only an itchy blue

stallion. He looked older. She went up to him and helped him scratch by nibbling at his back.

"Thanks – I rolled in ants and they bit me," he nickered. "Then… then I kinda got freaked out that I rolled in ants and I got hives too."

Cloudberry laughed in a horse way – which was kind of a soft neighing sound. The blue stallion tossed his head in annoyance.

Lorelei had seen the stallion's problem, and in the snap of two magical fingers, she concocted up a potion. She brought a bucket of it out and dropped it in front of the stallion.

"This should make your itching go away," said Lorelei. "Just drink some."

The stallion hesitantly lapped some of the purple liquid and then drank it. They all waited for a few minutes.

"Hey, I don't itch!" The stallion turned and hopped around like a Lipizzaner on a sugar high. Then he thanked everyone with a nicker (even Drake and Nellie) and danced off merrily.

"Well, well." said Valerie.

She had given Drake back the saddle pad, now clean and free of mold and mildew. It was quilted and very bright green. Too green.

"Whoa!" said Cloudberry. "It's… flashy."

"Yeah. And not moldy."

Drake got the saddle out and put it and the pad on her and tightened it slightly. They decided that Cloudberry should start getting used to it, so she could wear it for a little while. *At least it's not as weird feeling with the saddle pad on,* thought Cloudberry.

The stirrups bumped her sides. Drake did not know anything about English saddles so he didn't know how to put them up. Cloudberry was tickled.

"Hahhhh… hahhh… (twitch) HAHAAHHA (etc.)" Cloudberry took off and galloped madly into the forest. Then she came running out again and ran over to the house and ran all around until she stopped and Alidar came back and landed on her. Then she looked at him kindly because she didn't know he was a raven at the moment.

"Hello little bird!"

The bird seemed to enjoy standing on her rump.

"Alidar! Get off of Cloudberry's butt and come over here!" Valerie yelled.

Cloudberry bucked him off, squawking madly. *Well,* she thought, *at least it's easier to breathe with this saddle on than I thought…*

Lorelei turned Alidar back into unicorn, with a burst of steam, it appeared. "How did it go?" she asked.

"I found the sorry little house and dropped the letter on the doorstep," said Alidar. "And I flew over the racetrack by the portal and I wished I wasn't a bird because there were some really hot fillies running around. Besides that, your earth is lame, Drake."

Drake ignored the last comment. "Yeah, me and Nellie used to go watch races there all the time," said Drake. "That's how we came across the portal." He scratched his head absentmindedly and noticed his hair was getting pretty tall. "Man, I needed a haircut before I came here and I still do."

"NO Drake you should let your hair get longer so it'll flop over! It'll hide the acne on your ears!" Nellie said, and laughed.

Drake screeched at her and chased her around while Valerie laughed her head off.

Cloudberry was still nervous that night and she didn't want to sleep where they had been because she knew Nightcloud had probably swung by that area, if not only close to it. Maybe, she hoped, he wouldn't be brave enough to come near a human house. But that was unlikely.

Drake had taken the saddle off and Cloudberry had

sighed with gladness. He put it on the stand near the bridle hanging unused on the wall.

"You can sleep in Alidar's stall," said Valerie when they asked her about sleeping.

So when Alidar came into his stall for the night and saw Cloudberry there, lying with her legs curled to her side, he thought he got lucky. But then he saw Drake and Nellie. And snorted.

"Valerie said we could share the stall with you since Cloudberry's afraid of her brother," explained Drake.

Her brother? That must have been what she was freaked out about! I remember him! That crazy black colt that ran around being all secretive and stuff! Alidar thought. Everyone knew about that unicorn.

"You guys have to stay in the corner," Alidar said. "And GET YOUR GREASY PAWS OFF OF MY PILLOW!"

He seized the pillow from Nellie in his mouth and dropped it on the bedding near the wall. Then he took his blanket and laid down in the shavings.

"I thought that horses didn't lie down when they slept," Drake said.

"I'm not a horse. I'm a unicorn."

Drake leaned against Cloudberry's back for a pillow. He hoped she wouldn't roll over during the night.

"Cloudberry, do you wanna start practicing to get a jockey license tomorrow?"

"Yeah! I want to be a racehorse!"

Drake reached up to scratch her neck happily.

Alidar was listening. He felt sad. He didn't want her to be a racehorse... then, he would never get to see her, she'd be traveling to racetracks all the time – and he really did like her.

"After we win a bunch of money we can have our own house and you can eat the richest alfalfa and be known as the greatest race mare in the land." Drake put his arms behind his head.

"And my foals will be good racers too," said Cloudberry.

Alidar's lip got all quivery and his eyes got all teary since after all he was a real sensitive unicorn and he knew Cloudberry would never choose him as a mate. He pulled the covers up over his head with his teeth.

Nellie noticed Alidar tensing up, because she was very sharp on that kind of thing. "Drake. I can't sleep with you talking." She said.

"Okay... goodnight."

The next morning when they woke up, Alidar had already gotten up and left. The door was open.

I hope they get eaten by possums, Alidar had thought, having left an hour ago. *Well, everyone but Cloudberry...*

Cloudberry looked around then came out. She followed Drake to the house. "I wish I could fit in there," she said.

Drake had some funny puffy cereal that kind of resembled Cap'n Crunch only it was mostly purple.

"Hey Valerie. I'm going to get my jockey license soon," said Drake informatively.

"What?" She raised her eyebrows at him. "You don't even know where to get one," she said.

"At a racetrack..."

"Not just any racetrack!"

"Uhhh... Blaise will tell me where she got hers!"

Lorelei was cooking up some stuff on the kitchen counter. "Nonsense, you don't need to talk to that girl. The racetrack near here has jockey licenses. The only problem for you is they cost $50."

Drake groaned. More to add to his need for money. He needed racing saddle money and jockey license money and jockey clothes money...

"I guess we'll just have to win some of those cheap races," said Drake.

"Well, that's not so bad. If Alidar wasn't so small and slow we'd be racing him in them for fun."

Drake went back outside to Cloudberry. "Slight change of plans," he said. "First we must win $50 bucks in a cheap race before I can get a license. Since somehow they never mentioned that rule in the papers."

He got the saddle and bridle and he put the bridle on first. Then while Cloudberry was playing with the bit he put the saddle on tightly so it would not slide off. He took Cloudberry's left front leg and stretched it out in front of her, then the right one. Valerie had shown him how to do that because it got the pinches out of the girth area. Cloudberry looked at him strangely, and almost lost her balance the first time.

Drake had never ridden with a saddle before. He led Cloudberry over to a stump and used it as a mounting block. He put his right foot in the stirrup and stopped.

"Wait this isn't right…" he took it out and put his *left* foot in the stirrup. He hopped on lightly. When he had both feet in the stirrups he realized something wasn't right.

"The stirrups are different lengths…"

He jumped off and messed with the stirrups until he saw how to fix them. And he did, counting the number of holes so he would be accurate. He made them pretty long so he could step into them easier.

Finally he sat on the saddle correctly. (Well, not really... he slouched and his feet were jammed into the stirrups, and his heels were up!) So he went by the house and Valerie yelled, "*Put your heels down and sit up straight!!*"

Drake thought that he did while she came over. "You must keep your heels down because it makes it way easier to ride and you won't get your foot caught in the stirrup so easily if you fall. And if you slouch then you'll hurt your back." Valerie tried to explain the way to sit in the saddle but since she never rode with one she didn't really know herself. She only repeated what her sister had once told her.

Drake twisted around until he was sitting 'correctly' and he stayed like that. *Gosh, I feel like I should be wearing those riding tights right now,* he thought.

After Valerie told him how to post they trotted out onto the open grass and Drake tried until he figured it out. Cloudberry thought it felt odd, having a rider up there posting. A few days ago she never knew any humans, and now one was riding her!

Drake kept his heels down and his eyes up and told Cloudberry when to turn more with his body than his hands.

Cloudberry was annoyed with the bit, because it had lost its apple flavor. *Cheap thing,* she thought.

Cloudberry did her big, slow trot for a long while. They passed some herds of unicorns that looked at them warily as they passed, and they passed dragons, and Zenny, but they saw no evil black unicorns looking for revenge, thank goodness.

"Let's run," said Drake. He wanted to be like a jockey. Cloudberry jumped into a long-stridden gallop and Drake stood in the stirrups and pumped his hands madly. Cloudberry turned her head the slightest bit and looked at him funny.

There was a grazing ground up ahead with a few horses and a unicorn in it. The grass was short. It made Cloudberry want to tear it up… she went charging towards it.

Drake whooped. This was not a normal, by-your-self gallop. This was a flying, no-time-to-think-going-too-fast gallop, and there was no tall grass slowing Cloudberry down, and there were horses in front of her.

The horses (and unicorn!) heard her pounding hooves and looked up, wide eyed, and ran. Cloudberry chased one long-legged horse that was in front of her. She passed him, but he shied away sideways, afraid of Drake.

They galloped on until Cloudberry started to get tired

and Drake pulled the reins slightly to slow her. She walked willingly, her glowing coat darkened a little by sweat.

"You can run for so long! I know we'd whup anyone else in a long race," said Drake. "And if you got to sprinting then we could beat anyone, even Blaise's horse, because your strides are way bigger than hers."

"I'm ready," said Cloudberry. (She had finally gotten used to talking with a bit in her mouth, thank goodness.)

Drake suddenly felt a drop of rain on his head. He looked up. He had not noticed the light gray clouds floating around... when had *they* formed?

A raindrop fell on Cloudberry's hide, making a green spot. "Whoa!" said Drake. Cloudberry stopped.

"No I didn't mean stop I meant it's green! And there's an orange one... it's so Appaloosa-ie!"

"Yes..." said Cloudberry. Humans were so easily amused with color.

She pricked her ears as she saw the city off in the distance... she had been galloping a long time. "Hey, look," she said to Drake.

"A city? That must be where Valerie and Lorelei go to get groceries or something... maybe there's a racetrack near it."

"I think there is... but I'm not going to that crappy place. You'll never find me walking the streets in there."

"Well let's fly over the racetrack."

"I can't!"

"Oh yeah... the saddle. Well we can just find the racetrack and ignore the city, can't we?"

They started trotting towards the small buildings in the distance.

"Man, it looks just like a regular city," said Drake later as they approached it. It had some roads leading out of it and they went away into the horizon. A car went by on one. Cloudberry eyed it.

"There it is," Cloudberry said. Towards the end of the city the buildings thinned out a lot and there was more grass and then at the very end there was a track. They galloped for a while until they had gone past most of the city.

"Man. I wish I didn't have this saddle on so I could fly." Cloudberry said.

"Yeah, I know it's taking forever but we're almost there."

Cloudberry didn't like the way the polluted city smelled. She was glad she was a unicorn and not a human, so she didn't have to consider living there.

There was one horse facility. There were large pastures, and as Cloudberry passed, she saw horse showing at the edge of the buildings.

"Why would any horse or unicorn want to live there?"

Drake shrugged. "Maybe some don't like being wild."

They FINALLY made it to their destination, and Drake got off and led Cloudberry over to the track's office. They went in, Drake holding the door open for her. She looked up at the ceiling in awe, and looked around.

"Hello. Do you guys give jockey licenses?" Drake asked a lady behind the counter.

"No, we don't GIVE them, sweetie. But if you pass the test and pay $50 we'll sell you one," the lady behind the counter tapped her fingers together. "Now please get your unicorn out of here."

Drake grumbled and sent Cloudberry out. "I'll be back!" He said confidently as they left.

There were some dudes riding horses on the track. Jockey dudes. Drake watched them. Cloudberry gave them wary looks.

"Hey Cloudberry... let's go on the track!"

He got onto her back, and they went on the track and started trotting around. The jockeys and horses gave him odd looks. "Who are you?" one asked.

"I'm Drake and I'm going to be a jockey pretty soon." Drake said proudly.

"How do YOU know?" the guy asked challengingly. His mount looked at Cloudberry, as if sizing her up.

"Because Cloudberry's is really fast and I'm the right age and-"

"What? That unicorn? Are you kidding? She's gawkier looking than a newborn foal!" the dude pointed.

"Hey! I am not!" Cloudberry was P.Oed

"Oh, so you think otherwise?" the dude looked at her disapprovingly.

"YES! AND I'LL RACE YOUR HORSE AND KICK YOUR &^#@ (she learned that from Nellie) AND-"

"Okay okay! I would race you, but I'm only supposed to do a controlled gallop with Chully here today..." the guy reasoned.

"OH NO YOU DON'T," the filly shrieked.

Drake gulped and grabbed Cloudberry's mane. Cloudberry obviously had some work to do... she was tired, but angry. Drake had never seen her angry before. The rain that had been drizzling on her cooled her and made her coat look like she had been in an accident with a rainbow.

'Chully', the colt the dude was riding bounced on his hindquarters. He was a dark bay, had no horn, and a short

216

cropped little mane. He was definitely ready to race even if the jockey didn't want to.

Drake noticed that some other jockeys had been watching, when he heard someone yell gleefully, "On your marks, ponies – get set, go!"

They went exploding around the track, dodging the other horses and screeching jockeys/exercise riders. Cloudberry felt very powerful, as if she was fresh, and she dug in, leaving the colt behind. Many of the other horses running bounced to run after her as she passed, tails raising excitedly. The sound of arguing came to the track, between a few bouncy racehorses and gruff jockeys.

All the humans were screeching madly at them. The one they were 'racing' was left behind. They passed trainers standing on the side of the track, and some were cussing at them, shaking their fists, and some were looking at their timers.

"Cloudberry, I think we'd better go," said Drake. They had galloped all the way around the track (it was a small track) and it was probably time to go home… Cloudberry slowed down and jumped over the small railing, her neck extending. She galloped for the open plains. Drake hadn't expected the jump until the last moment, but he was already leaning forward with a death grip on the mane so he didn't fly off the back or anything and get trampled by angry racehorses, thank goodness.

They cantered for a while, until Cloudberry was too tired to keep going speedy. She walked. Her head drooped and she dragged her feet from being tired, but she was proud – she had shown that jockey, all right. The rain still drizzled down on them.

Drake had an idea. Dismounting, he took her saddle and pad off. Then he tightened the saddle as tight as it would go (which was still very loose) around his waist and folded the pad up and put it in his pocket. He folded that pad thirty four times to get it to fit.

Anyone who passed would be confused to see a person wearing a saddle but the only ones around were other horses and birds. Drake got on Cloudberry's sweaty and now saddle-less back.

"You can fly now!" he said.

Her wings flapped out thankfully, and they flew all the way back. Cloudberry wanted to rest, but had not forgotten about Nightcloud. She grazed watchfully near the house.

"There you are! My gosh, you were gone FOR EVER! What were you doing?" asked Nellie, finding them in front of the house.

"We found a racetrack," said Drake. Then he told her all about the city and everything, and she was surprised.

"I want to see the city... dang. That's so cool. I wonder what Uni's cities are like... I want to go there with you guys. Soon."

"Okay... but Cloudberry's real tired so you might have to ride Alidar."

Outside, the rain was getting heavier. Cloudberry kept grazing, and then went into Alidar's stall. There was a water bucket in there. Happily, she drank. Then she lay down to rest her legs.

Alidar was coming in for shelter from the rain. He saw Cloudberry lying there hogging all the space. He had been thinking about it and now he was trying to be a manly horse again.

"Are you okay?" he asked, his eyes getting that gentle, concerned look again.

"Zzzzzzz."

D'oh, thought Alidar.

He went over to his water bucket, and saw that it was empty. He sighed. Cloudberry's eyes popped open.

"Hey Alidar." She greeted, raising her head slightly. "What are you doing sneaking around here?"

"Nothing! Just getting out of the rain..." he said quickly.

She moved over. "Well I'll be lying here," she said. "If you leave, close the door."

He looked at her for a few seconds. "I'll stay here." he lay down near Cloudberry with his legs folded under him.

Oh yeah, I've got it, he thought, enjoying the nearness of her. "So what do you like to do in your spare time?"

"Zzzzzzzz."

He sighed.

Chapter 9

Cloudberry the Racehorse

There was a black form of a unicorn… it moved through the grass silently. It was going towards the forest. A house was nestled innocently at the edge. Its body tense, the animal whinnied angrily.

Cloudberry woke. Her head jerked up. She pricked her ears. Had she heard a whinny, or had it been her dream…?

Alidar had been sleeping next to her romantically

(well, *he* thought it was) and he got shifted slightly when Cloudberry's head went up. He woke up.

"Wha…" he said grumpily.

Drake was awake too. "What is it, Cloudberry?"

"I had a dream Nightcloud was coming." she said.

"So? It was just a dream," said Nellie, trying to be reassuring.

"Dreams mean things," said Cloudberry. "I must be careful now. He was very angry."

"Well tomorrow, we'll probably be over checking out those cheap races," said Drake. "Maybe we'll win a race!"

"You *know* we will," said Cloudberry lightheartedly.

Outside, it was still dark. There were stars in the sky. The night air came into the stall through the open top half of the door. Cloudberry looked out nervously until Alidar got up and went over to pull a curtain down from the top of the doorway. It covered the window, but the moonlight still shone through.

"There. Now no one can see in here," said Alidar.

"Thanks, Alidar… I didn't know you had a curtain." She touched noses with him as he came back over, a gesture of friendship

The rest of the night she was able to sleep. She had odd dreams, so she was a bit confused when she woke up.

Drake was gentle with her and he said there was no pressure on her to stay around if she was frightened... he knew she'd come back. But she said she wanted to stay with him, and race. Drake planned to try and find the 'cheap races' that day. Cloudberry said she was ready. Her tail raised a little.

He had not been feeding her since she grazed so much, but now she was using a lot of energy and he needed to give her food. Valerie let him borrow some of Alidar's oats.

Why didn't I think of that before? He wondered.

He put the oats in a bucket and set it in front of Cloudberry. She sniffed it. "What is this?"

"It's food. It'll give you more strength than grass. Go ahead and dig in, Alidar eats it."

Cloudberry chomped the oats happily.

Inside the house, Lorelei gave him directions to the race-tracks. It was not too far, but it was in the opposite direction of the city and they would need to go through part of the forest. A thin part, not the dangerous part Lorelei had warned them of when they first came.

"Drake, I want to come with you," said Nellie. "I'll get Alidar to let me ride him."

"Okay."

"What about me?" asked Valerie. "I want to watch you race too. And Alidar is my horse."

"Well we could ride double," suggested Nellie.

"NOOOOOOOOOOOOO!" Alidar was listening through the window. "I HATE DOUBLE!"

"You want to watch?" asked Drake, surprised.

"Sure, I need a day off from this magical stuff anyway."

"Well then... I guess I'll have to ride Cloudberry double with Nellie since there's no one for her to ride... but then I couldn't ride with a saddle because it's too small for both of us. I'll have to race bareback."

"You can hold on to the mane," Nellie reminded. "And if you fall off and get trampled then at least we'll still have Cloudberry."

Drake ulped even though she was only joking.

"I'll tell you guys if we're going in the wrong direction," said Valerie.

Soon they started off, Cloudberry carrying Drake and Nellie bareback, and Alidar carrying Valerie. Valerie was riding with a towel on Alidar, so he wouldn't get sweaty and make her slide off. Cloudberry now preferred having two people riding to a saddle. Saddle 'butts' were hard.

Valerie was in the lead as they went through the forest, avoiding some trees, as it seemed to Drake, for no reason at all. He figured they must be magical portal trees or something.

The trees thinned out soon and there was more grass. The sun was hot on their heads, but a cool breeze ruffled their hair and manes (and tails).

"I thought that the forest was thicker," said Drake.

"It is very thick. We just went through a thin part. The forest is shaped funny." Then she added, "Up ahead the ground is going to start getting rougher and hillier. We call it the rocks."

"Oh. I wondered if this place was all grass or not." Drake looked around at the green hills.

"Look, there's a unicorn," Nellie pointed out a few minutes later.

They all looked up and there was a unicorn gliding across the sky. It was a dappled gray mare. Alidar whinnied.

The unicorn whinnied back and Alidar was about to get into a whinnying match with it when he tripped over a rock and fell over. Valerie jumped off of him.

"Are you all right?" she asked, leaning down in fear.

"No. I've been stabbed through the heart by a stick. Hopefully I'll have recovered when that mare flies away." Alidar mumbled.

He got up embarrassedly and found what he had tripped on. A rock.

"It was YOU ya son of a-" he started at it.

"Well I guess we made it to the rocks," said Valerie, cutting him off. "See all the sand starting to appear."

They walked along in the hills, Cloudberry finding patches of sand to avoid the rocks. She knew this place, of course, and she had gone through it times before in her wild travels, but once she had gotten a stone bruise, and it had hurt her for a long time, since her hooves were not made to navigate rocky ground. She must be careful or Drake would not be able to ride her if she was injured. She wanted to fly. But she really didn't know if she could fly with two humans on her back. That would be a challenge...

"Can we fly now?" said Alidar before her.

"I don't know if I can fly with two riders..." Cloudberry said

"*I* can do it! You can do it too providing you don't mind someone sitting on your rump!"

Cloudberry flapped her wings out, but Drake and Nellie were ready this time and already sitting far back. So they would NOT fly off and land on a rock painfully!

While they were flying, Drake was holding Cloudberry's mane and Nellie was holding Drake's mane but unfortunately it was too short and he went "OUCH" so she held onto his shirt instead. She refused to put her arms around him.

Soon in the distance there was a speck. Valerie pointed it out. "It's the town. The track is close by."

The terrain turned back into grass near the town. They landed and broke into canters toward it. Like the city, it had roads going off into the horizon. But it was small and more country-like. There were no buildings that were very tall. Cloudberry spotted some horses and unicorns walking around in it.

They walked on the side of the road in the town. No one was driving today. All the cars were in the garages and people were riding horses and unicorns around. Drake had noticed that the roads in Uni were made of something slightly softer than pavement, so the horses would not hurt their hooves on them.

Not too far into the town there was break of buildings, and a huge grass field. The border around the field was sand and it looked like a racetrack. Inside the field there were many horses and people, another riding ring with colorful and unfamiliar jumps inside of it, and there were horses showing.

"The track goes all the way around the field," said Valerie. "Here come some horses."

Some horses wearing Western, English, and all other sorts of un-jockey like saddles and jeans-wearing riders galloped by. They were running really fast. Drake gulped at the thought of him falling off in that mess. He didn't like to show worry, but….

"It looks like there is going to be another race soon so we should go sign up." Valerie said.

"That soon?" Drake looked at the closed gate. But the way in is through the track. And it's closed."

A bell rung announcing the end of the race and the gates on the side of the track opened. They went in, Drake feeling rather dim.

There were lots of people and horses there, and Cloudberry shuddered as a fat pinto brushed by her. But it was exciting, and her heart was going… she looked around. She could beat these horses… they all looked round-bellied and short.

"Don't underestimate these guys," said Drake. "They may look slow, but stocky horses can sprint real fast and they'll probably blow your doors off in the start."

They walked up to a table with a sign that said entries. The guy behind the counter eyed them.

"I haven't seen you folks around here before… are you entering a race?"

Valerie spoke. "Yes, my friend wants to enter."

Drake and Nellie got off of Cloudberry and Drake was given a pen and some papers to sign. Where to begin? He selected the quarter-mile race in the list of races. It wasn't Cloudberry's distance, but he figured it was a good start. If he won he would get $50.

He ulped as he signed under a paragraph saying that he would not charge Gold Ring park if he fell off and suffered injury or died.

"That'll be $5 bucks."

"What?"

Valerie handed Drake $5 bucks to save his sorry hide.

"Oh. Thanks."

"The race is in about 15 minutes. It'll come over the PA to get ready." the man said, turning away to take someone else's fee.

They strolled over to the jumping ring and watched. Cloudberry was looking around at everything and everyone with interest. There were so many different people and mounts… all the horses and unicorns looked fancy, not like the wild horses. They wore all different types of saddles.

Cloudberry didn't understand the jumping, but she thought it looked pretty. There was a sleek dappled gray hornless horse, its mane bunched into little bunches somehow, gracefully jumping over brightly painted jumps, with flowers and all sorts of funny things stuck to them. The jumps were tall. The horse jumping looked good, but it ended up with an odd distance, jumping late on one, letting its back hooves clip on the jump, causing a blue and white rail to fall down.

"Too bad," said Nellie.

The rider flicked her crop on the horse's shoulder, and it cantered faster, trying to make up lost time from the rail penalty, but their concentration was broken and they knocked over two more rails before they finished the course.

"I'm going to go bet on the race," said Valerie, walking off.

"Huh?" Drake had not been paying attention. "Who are you betting on?"

"That guy with the piebald paint."

"Thanks for being supportive," mumbled Drake. "We'll show her, won't we Cloudberry?"

Cloudberry was watching Alidar flirt with an unsaddled mare tied to a post.

"So, are you a show halter mare or are you not saddled yet?" he asked.

"You can ask my boyfriend right there."

Alidar looked over and gulped. The bay stud snorted at him in annoyance and he ran.

Cloudberry nickered and Alidar came over. "Why don't

you race? If you won, then the mares probably wouldn't think you're a creep."

"They don't think I'm a creep…" Alidar protested.

"If they thought you were hot, then they'd be following you around."

"Besides, I can't win a race!"

"Why not?"

"Because… because I'm too small!"

"You're not too small… no one's too small to win a race if they try hard enough."

"You just say that because you're big."

"You run every day. You only lose because you don't think you can win. You have no confidence." Cloudberry shook her mane.

Alidar sneaked away at the embarrassment of a mare telling him he had no confidence. But it was true… he was a wimpy horse. He got all emotional and went and found Valerie.

"Valerie."

"Hmm?" she touched his neck.

"I want to enter a race so I won't be a wimpy horse." he continued.

"What? Who said you were a wimpy horse?"

"Cloudberry."

"Well… I guess she was kind of telling the truth."

She giggled and Alidar glared at everything within his range of vision.

"attention… race number three is about to begin. contestants come to the starting line."

Drake gulped. He climbed onto Cloudberry, thankful that he hadn't fallen off again in public, and they started making their way to the line of horses on the track.

Nellie, Valerie, and Alidar went to wait at the finish line, which was at the end of a straight stretch of the track a quarter mile long.

"What on earth are you doing riding with no saddle?" An English riding girl with a light gray horse looked at Drake like he was nuts.

He ignored the comment and went onto the track. They were next to last to line up, and they were on the outside. A bad place to be in a race with turns, but this was a straight race so it was okay. Drake held on to Cloudberry's mane. There would be no need to steer her in this race, so he let the reins hang loosely.

The dun next to them snorted and pawed at the ground, his weight on his hindquarters. Cloudberry did the same, ready to jump forward. The announcer was calling…

"On your marks… get set…" A horn blew loudly and

the horses shot forward. Cloudberry was quickly put behind horses – their 'jockeys' were hissing, kicking and going wild to encourage their mounts. Cloudberry sprinted as fast as she could – she tried to make her strides smaller like the other horses. Towards the end she started passing the others, and she managed to get her nose over the finish line in 3rd place.

They slowed and followed the other horses out of the track. Nellie and Valerie came over to greet them.

"That was great! Another few yards and you would have blown them away," said Nellie encouragingly.

"And the one I betted on won," said Valerie, smiling (Drake suspected) even bigger than she would have if Cloudberry had won.

Drake rolled his eyes and patted Cloudberry, who was jigging around excitely. "Drake, can we race again? I want to race again!" she said hyperly.

"Of course! Let's enter another!"

"Are you sure?" Valerie asked both of them. "You might get tired out…"

"Oh, we gallop more than this every day!"

"Well. You guys should probably go over there and enter, then… I think the half mile race is your best bet."

They decided to race in the half mile race, in another

hour and 25 minutes. Valerie paid for their entry again. Cloudberry rested under the trees, though she was happy and excited. "I know I can beat those guys," she said. "I'll out-run them next time."

Alidar came over and waited next to her. Drake had managed to borrow an extra buck, had bought a hot dog from the food stand and was eating it in the grass. Valerie was off somewhere doing something and Nellie was watching the horses in the ring nearby.

"Are you going to race, Alidar?" Cloudberry asked slyly.

"No!" he had changed his mind when he watched the race. His rare brave moment was gone...

"You're so boring."

Alidar was offended. He "humphed" and stomped off. Cloudberry grazed the odd tasting grass.

Later, after they had gotten pretty bored of standing there waiting, Drake looked at his watch and saw that it was almost time for the race. He hopped up onto Cloudberry, and they pranced over to the track again. Cloudberry turned a lot of heads. *Of course she's prettier than all these horses,* Drake thought.

Unfortunately, Cloudberry noticed, the horses she was racing this time were better looking than the last ones. *Bigger strides,* she thought when she saw them.

"Drake I'm going to bet on you this time in hopes of getting my $10 bucks back so you'd better win. Or I'll turn your hair purple!!"

Hmm... that'd be awesome, thought Drake of purple hair. *But I'm still going to win anyway!*

They waited close to the starting line until the announcer called. There were other horses waiting too, and they beat them to the rail and managed to be the 4th horse in the lineup. This race, since longer, started out on a turn and ended on the straightaway.

Drake looked to his right. There was some redneck cowboy on a black mare. He looked to the left. There was some girl on a long skinny horse that looked like a Tennessee walking horse with a horn on its head. Probably a Staperville Walking Unicorn. He increased his death grip on the mane and leaned forward dramatically.

Cloudberry looked over sideways at the handsome walking horse but she snapped back when the announcer began counting down. The starting horn blew, and the horses charged forward.

Drake was thrown a little sideways at the angle of the track and for a moment he had a heart attack and squeezed Cloudberry. She went flying forward. She was not out sprinted as badly this time and soon she started to pass the other horses. There was still a group of horses in front of her, but she found a way through them and passed them. The walking horse was ahead now. They were almost halfway done with the race. Suddenly Cloudberry couldn't leave the other horses behind as fast, and she realized they had been pacing themselves. She wasn't nearly tired, though. She put out a spurt of speed and she passed the walking horse in seconds. Drake felt the other horses trying to come at them and he urged Cloudberry on with his arms. She wasn't running full speed, but she didn't need to. She crossed the finish line about 7 feet in front of the second placer.

Drake whooped in victory, even as they trotted off of the track. He found Valerie and Nellie waiting again.

Guys, thought Nellie as Drake struck a pose. They pranced away to get their $50 bucks.

"All right, so we can go now, right?" said Valerie when they came back. And she snatched two of Drake's $5 dollar bills. "Thanks for paying me back."

"I need to buy a helmet with this," Drake said jokingly. I thought I was gonna die out there for a moment."

Drake and Nellie agreed that they were done, as well as Cloudberry and Alidar, and they went out while the gates were still open and they soon had walked out of town.

"Alidar, you should have raced, you scaredy cat." Cloudberry teased.

Suddenly, she stopped as her hooves touched rocks and she pricked her ears. She stretched her neck out and looked up. There were ominous looking clouds in the sky... she sniffed the air.

"What is it?" asked Drake.

"I thought I smelled him... my brother," said Cloudberry.

"Nightcloud?" said Nellie.

Cloudberry was hesitant, but Alidar flapped his wings out hurriedly. "It's a storm coming, from over there," he said. "We have to hurry up and get home..."

Cloudberry felt a little better; maybe Nightcloud – if he was here – wouldn't come near if her humans were there. She flew along with Alidar until they were over the grass again and landed. There was wind blowing towards the storm, which was swelling dangerously. The sky was dark over there. Suddenly they saw a lightning flash, and heard thunder... but wait, it wasn't thunder.

Nightcloud – it was definitely him – galloped past them at cruising speed about 80 feet in front of them. His hooves pounded the ground rhythmically but wildly. He didn't seem to see them.

Cloudberry stopped, and Drake and Nellie bumped into each other and onto her neck. Nellie looked. Drake could not look since he was smooshed into Cloudberry's mane.

Nightcloud continued running off into the distance, a blue-black streak of flying hooves.

"He's so pretty," said Nellie sadly. "And so darn fast!"

"Well, I'm glad he didn't see us... or maybe he did, but he's running from something..." Cloudberry commented.

Suddenly, they heard more thunder – but it was just hoof beats again, and a huge herd of unicorns came stampeding past them. They wanted to get away from that storm fast.

"Ice!" said Valerie suddenly. "There must be hail and ice in the storm! We need to get our butts home."

They started galloping towards the speck in the distance that was the forest. They were right about one thing, the horses were running from the storm. It was coming closer very fast. They could hear the thunder, and they knew they would be like lightning rods out there in the plains.

Cloudberry was running slow, because she was tired and Drake and Nellie were weighing her down, and Alidar was running fast, but since he was smaller they were pretty much running the same speed. However, they made it into the forest just as the rain started to sprinkle on them. Lorelei was waiting on the porch for them, and Nellie and Valerie jumped off of the unicorns and went inside. Drake jumped off of Cloudberry and they hurried over to the stall, and he took off Cloudberry's bridle and put it in the tack shed. Lightning flashed. Drake waved and ran to the house, as the rain poured and hail started thumping on the roof of the stall.

Alidar closed the top half of his door. It was dark in the stall until he found his light switch, high in the corner of the stall and turned on the light bulb in the ceiling.

"Hey, you have a light bulb in here," said Cloudberry, looking at it with perked ears. Drake and she had somehow already had a conversation about where human light came from other than fires, so she knew the words.

"Well, yes, of course." Alidar replied.

"What if you reared and zapped yourself on it or something?"

"Why would I do that?"

Meanwhile, the humans were all sitting around inside the house. "The weather changed fast," said Drake. "Does it always do that?"

"No, not usually that fast. This is a bad storm." Lorelei had a purple drink. She sipped it. "I hope the hail doesn't hurt anyone too bad... or I'll have a lot of patients coming around tomorrow."

"What do the cloud unicorns do during storms?" asked Drake.

"Their clouds rise up above the storm." The purple haired sorceress replied.

"Let's watch television..." Valerie cut in, and turned on some judge what's-her-face show.

"I'm going to look in this newspaper," said Drake, picking up a newspaper.

"That's not a newspaper. We don't get newspapers."

"Whoa..." Drake set the paper down in horror. It definitely was not a newspaper.

Lorelei snatched her paper away. "That's my spell ingredients page!"

"I'm never going to let you make me food again, after handling that!" Drake said.

Meanwhile (AGAIN) the unicorns were huddled together in the stall. Some thunder banged right above them, and they jumped in fear.

"Do you think we're going to get struck by lightning?" Cloudberry asked fearfully.

"I don't know, I've never been…" Alidar started.

"Maybe your light bulb will attract the electricity and fry us!"

"AACK!!" Alidar ran about two steps and turned the light off. It was dark (and scary!) and he flung himself back into Cloudberry. She grunted in surprise. "Sorry, I thought I lost you." Alidar said sheepishly.

Cloudberry sighed.

While all that was happening in the barn, a CERTAIN black unicorn was hiding – no, he hid from nothing, so he was *sheltering* – under the trees in a small forest. The forest was not the one Lorelei lived in – it was barely even big enough to be called a forest.

The lightning struck close. Nightcloud winced with the thunder and sunk deeper into the trees. He saw a lone pine get zapped – not far away at all. It burst into flames and fell.

Nightcloud backed a little more, and his rump bumped into another horse. He whirled around.

"Watch where you're backing!" snarled a palomino colt, moving away.

Nightcloud pinned his ears, giving him a furious look, and took no hesitation to kick at the palomino until he skittered away, nickering angrily to himself.

Nightcloud glared after him.

It was pouring, but the canopy of treetops above them was thick. Still, Nightcloud's glossy black coat was wet. He twitched his skin unhappily. There was a band of other horses and unicorns in the trees nearby, but they kept their distance... he didn't like their company.

I must find Cloudberry tomorrow, he thought, his brain working like clockwork, repetitive. It was as if he was going over the same things. *She disappeared today, and by the time I saw her I was running from the hail... I have to find her again. She deserves it... she'll feel the wrath one way or another...*

A wayward young painted stallion had drifted in front of Nightcloud. Annoyed, he reached out and nipped the fat spotted rump. The pinto shied in surprise and tried to nip Nightcloud's shoulder in return, thinking he might have been playing or challenging, but the black stallion reared up and fought him off with his front hooves. He bared his teeth threateningly. A small bit of glossy, wet feathers on the backs of his fetlocks seemed to make him look a bit thicker, and the painted stallion backed away.

Nightcloud blew through nostrils and pawed the ground in anger. How dare anyone fight back with him... he could beat this horse to the death, if he had a mind to. He wasn't leaving fast enough.

Nightcloud lunged at him in annoyance, and the horse scrambled backwards onto his hindquarters and sat, the white rings around his eyes making him look more scared than he already was. Nightcloud stopped, held his head high, looking down his nose at him, and let him get back up and trot away. He shook his long mane, which fell on both sides of his neck unevenly like Cloudberry's. It was mostly on his unlucky right side, and there were a few wisps on the left.

There was thunder crashing out there... he suddenly felt something hit the top of his tender muzzle and fall to the ground. It was a shard of ice. He crushed it with his hoof.

"@#$!%ing..." Nightcloud didn't get a chance to say any more dirty words because more hail started coming through the hole in the leafy ceiling. Nightcloud turned and trotted even farther into the 'forest'. A hailstone bounced off of his back – he only thought with pleasure of the bite he had left on Cloudberry.

He had hated her – ever since his mother had left him alone to go birth her, and then had almost seemed to forget he existed. Never again was he even heard until he was a yearling, and she led him out to the high, high top of the cloud and left him. Why, he wondered, had he been abandoned while the other foals had remained by their mothers long after they had other foals? And why had she taken him and left him on the very top of that cloud, whinnied to the skies, and disappeared? *Oh yes,* he thought, *she wanted me dead… she wanted to be rid of my black hide, didn't she. That is the reason the other colts hated and fought with me, so why wouldn't she…*

But in his heart he knew it was not that. Most likely, he would never know… he blamed Cloudberry for all he didn't know. He must get revenge on her… his mind was clouded with that idea. Sure, he knew he was crazy, had known since he had fallen all the way down from that cloud, knowing in no way how he had possibly survived and woken up in the land below. He didn't care. He was living his life that he had almost been denied, and he thought he was doing a pretty good job of it. He had a goal. A dark one at that, but it was still a goal.

He suddenly whickered a laugh to himself, and the other horses and unicorns that were near him scooted further away.

Chapter 10

The Climactic Scene

When Cloudberry woke the next morning, she was even stiffer than before.

She groaned and stretched, her muscles sore. Alidar was lying next to her. He raised his head, and nickered softly.

"I'm all sore," she said. "Shouldn't have run so much and then stood still..."

She heard footsteps outside. Drake opened and peeked in the bottom half of the door. He grinned slyly.

"Oh, I'm sorry to wake you two love birds."

Cloudberry rose and opened the top half of the door, bonking Drake's head.

"Ow."

"I'm kind of stiff today," the filly said. "I don't know if I can run."

"Well, we won't go back to the racetrack until you're ready. We can rest today. I'm not in a hurry to win," Drake assured, though he did want to get his jockey license soon.

"I'll walk around," said Cloudberry. "It would probably be too muddy from the storm anyway."

Outside, it was sunny and damp. There were no clouds in the sky, except for the cumulus-like unicorn clouds. The real ones had all passed. Drake gave Cloudberry a bucket of oats, and she plunged her muzzle into it hungrily. She had hardly grazed yesterday... only while waiting for the races.

Alidar came out and squealed at her for eating HIS oats. But Drake had some for Alidar too, oats that Valerie told Drake to give to him. Cloudberry finished long before Alidar and walked around, stretching her legs. The air was clear... her pearly white coat glowed. All except for the bald, pain-ful-looking bite mark on her rump. It was healing, though. It reminded her that Nightcloud would be watching her... but she didn't think he would come today, not after seeing him fleeing yesterday. He must be far away by now.

"Drake, I want to come with you to ride Cloudberry to-day," said Nellie.

"We're just walking."

"That's fine."

Drake gave Cloudberry time and then got her bridle out. He put it on her and brushed her with all the different brush-es... not a very manly thing to do, he thought, but he secretly liked making her all pretty like that.

She lipped and pricked her ears at something in the distance. She looked odd with that pearly white skin...

"Hey, that dragon is here." She said.

Zenny ambled on the pathway to the house. *Some things never change...* thought Drake.

"Hello, Zenny," Nellie said, greeting him.

"Drake and I are about to go riding."

"Oh. Have you raced yet?" the dragon asked. Maybe Lorelei or Valerie had told him about their plans at the recent breakfast.

"Yes, Drake and Cloudberry got a 3rd place and a 1st so far."

So far. Drake thought about it... soon he and Cloudberry would go back to the track and race until he had enough money to get his license, then his silks, and his racing saddle... they would be racing. He would be a jockey! Then, when they had all that and were racing officially, Drake could win the Kentucky Derby – wait, no he could win the UNI Derby. He couldn't exactly take a unicorn back to earth, due to what Lorelei had said about that, if he ever even could go back.

When would Lorelei trust him? Would she tell him?

They would win a ton of money in no time and build a house. When Cloudberry retired, a millionaire racehorse, she could have foals, and Drake would raise them and win more races on them… but that was far in the future, he thought.

He was in daydreaming mode again. He brushed the same spot on Cloudberry until it was so clean it was scary, and she looked around at him in confusion.

"Oh. Sorry."

"You guys are going to go without me?" said Alidar, seeing them get ready to leave.

"Yeppers."

"Are you suddenly lonely?" asked Nellie, who had come back over.

"Well, uh, no…"

Drake grabbed Cloudberry's mane and hoisted himself onto her back. He had gotten much better at it, finally. He leaned to the right and Nellie grabbed his arm and jumped up behind him. Cloudberry grunted, but since being ridden a lot, she didn't mind the weight too much anymore.

"Lorelei, we're going on a walk," Drake called into the house. She waved from the kitchen.

They walked out into the open, the grass tickling Cloudberry's legs in a way that she knew she was where she needed to be. Something about seeing the grass in front of her, the ground stretching flat into the horizon, made her want to run, so, so fast.

She must rest today. She walked out into the open plains, the breeze blowing her long mane. It blew Drake's fuzzy hair over. He felt it. Well, girls liked guys with long flowing hair anyway…

Nellie was wearing jeans and a yellow halter top today. Her black hair was shiny and curly as usual, and it reached halfway down her back. Her hair was her pride and joy!

She now always wondered if she would find a horse or unicorn for her own. Nightcloud was beautiful, but he was wild and crazy, too. Maybe she should give up on finding a true black horse and settle for a chestnut that she had seen galloping pretty fast out with Sunridge's herd.

Cloudberry forgot she was resting and started to trot. "Cloudberry…" Drake said.

She slowed and pranced, her neck arched. Drake heard some hoof beats. Blaise and Songoffire galloped by in the distance. Blaise waved and winked at Drake, before turning away from them and disappearing into the green.

"Why, that…" Nellie mumbled and Drake, like any typical guy, drooled.

They walked for a long time. They walked past the city. Nellie looked at it and it didn't seem too different than any regular city.

Cloudberry was going strong under them, a little sweaty, but her white coat wasn't too hot.

"Maybe we should turn back," said Drake after a little while. Some more clouds had come and drifted towards them in the sky. "Remember how fast that storm came yesterday."

"I wonder where it all went," said Nellie.

"To the sea," said Cloudberry. "It's probably a choppy day out in the ocean. It isn't too far ahead."

"I still think we should go back…" said Drake worriedly. But then again, he had never been to the beach in Uni…

Cloudberry turned around, ready to go back, but she stopped and raised her head, pricking her ears.

"What is it?" asked Drake.

A long, shrill whinny came from the direction they had come. Nightcloud, but a black speck in the distance, reared challengingly. He struck at the ground and began to gallop towards them.

"He was following us," said Cloudberry, shuddering. "I've got to run!"

She turned and started to gallop away, Drake and Nellie holding on, but she was slow carrying the two humans. Nellie looked back at Nightcloud, charging straight for them. He bugled a challenge, jumping a few strides, and seemed to slow down. There was no use in wasting his energy... he would wait for her to tire. His head was high.

Afraid, Cloudberry ran with her head down and legs flying. She started to turn, but she saw Nightcloud out of the corner of her eye threaten to block her way. He drove her straight.

Drake and Nellie encouraged Cloudberry, but they didn't know what to do... they had nothing to throw at Nightcloud or anything. They could only hold on. And somehow, they didn't think yelling or waving their arms was going to scare this unicorn away.

Nightcloud smelled Cloudberry's scent, strong, in front of him. He did not advance on her, he just drove her on. He snorted with every stride, his breathing hard and excited.

Nellie looked back again. Surprisingly, Nightcloud looked right back at her with an expression of annoyance. *What a nuisance, those humans,* thought Nightcloud. *Right now they are slowing her and will undoubtedly be the cause of her pain. Why would a unicorn give themselves to a human?*

Nellie noticed his eyes were a bluish-purple color. Very pretty with his black coat... but they were angry and not quite sane eyes at the moment. Rather frightening.

Up ahead, Cloudberry saw the grass thin out and the ground drop off to sand... the sea. The top line was ridged, steep, and hilly near one side. There was a large, jagged cliff, with a steep right side going down, and beside it there was beach... soft, white sand. The waves were high, and the swirling gray waters were scary looking... off in the distance, where the ocean met the sky, there were gray clouds.

Cloudberry slowed. Nightcloud would drive her right off of that cliff! She was nearing it so rapidly, with nowhere else to turn to without him cutting her off. She felt his hot breath on her flank, and he nipped her hocks. She squealed at him, suddenly knowing to go no further, and Drake and Nellie both toppled off. Nightcloud snorted angrily at them. They weren't hurt, luckily, a bit bruised, but they ran to the side, away from the unicorns.

Cloudberry would not leave the humans there... she must stay and fight. Nightcloud reared and pawed when she balked, and drove her out onto the cliff. For a moment she considered flapping her wings out and flying away, but Nightcloud could injure her easily in the air and her wings could be crippled.

She reared, whinnying angrily in retaliation, and struck at Nightcloud, but it only made him more furious and he knocked her legs out from under her as she reared. She fell onto the hard ground painfully and Nightcloud reared above her, ready to strike, but she sprung back up as his hooves hit the dirt. He reared again in surprise, and she half-reared, pounding him in the belly with her two front hooves.

He made a gasping noise and went back down, but only to swiftly stab at her with his sharp, black horn. He jabbed her shoulder once, and she seized the crest of his neck and tried to throw him off balance. But feeling as strong as he ever would, the black forced her over instead, grabbing for her throat.

She squealed in fear and hit the ground. Nightcloud reared triumphantly. "It is for all you have caused me," he said. "This is what you deserve!"

She rolled away as he tried to stomp on her once more. Given the chance, he could very well pound his unforgiving hooves into her body and neck... she must live, she must become a racehorse, Drake's unicorn.

Her horn made a deep gash on Nightcloud's chest as she got up, flinging her head at him. He squealed once in pain and rage, backing a small step absently. Cloudberry rushed at him, leaping up to pound at him with her fore hooves again. He was knocked over to the ground.

He squealed in anger and panic as she pawed the ground by him threateningly, but she wasn't cruel or brave enough to do anything to him. She immediately regretted it. He got up, the filly whirling around behind him so his horn was away from her, and he kicked at her with his back legs.

Drake and Nellie were watching fearfully. Bloody gashes had appeared on both of the unicorns. One of them would lose the fight soon. Nightcloud was stronger than Cloudberry, and quicker, but he was tiring, as she was, drained from running the day before.

Drake yelled, his face white, "Watch out Cloudberry! You're getting close to the edge! Don't get close to the edge!" but he wasn't sure if she could even hear.

They screamed angrily at each other and bit and kicked. Nightcloud aimed for Cloudberry's throat area, but she blocked him each time. They reared together, striking with their forelegs. Then they crashed into each other, each trying to get to the other's weak points.

Cloudberry fell away, and she dug her hooves into the ground in fear. She was so close to the edge, she must not go back any further or she would fall to the water below.

Nightcloud squealed, blind with fury, and he did not think... he flung himself at Cloudberry, successfully sending her backwards. Off the cliff's edge, which he had planned to be close. He had fought her, driving her steadily towards that edge she'd go off of to her death. What he didn't plan was going with her.

Nellie and Drake both yelled at the same time, "No!" Nellie put her hands over her mouth to keep from making more sound.

Cloudberry was pushed outward by the force of Nightcloud. For a dizzying moment, she was alone in the air. Then a sickening snap sliced through the silence as Nightcloud himself hit rock on the side of the cliff... Cloudberry heard another thud as his body was slammed into a rock at the bottom, and then the two hit the water, Cloudberry making a splash.

The water was cold and quiet, except for the faint sounds of the crashing waves at the beach. Cloudberry's eyes wide, she pushed back up to the surface, snorting out water and trying to keep her head above the choppy whitecaps. The beach! She must get to the beach before she was thrown into the rocks by a wave!

She heard a terrified, waterlogged squeal behind her. Her ears flicked back in surprise. Nightcloud... Nightcloud was alive! She turned her head, struggling to see him. Only his face was visible, as he was struggling and bobbling in the water, the rest of him submerged. The current threatened to suck him under, and he could not swim because he was injured somehow, Cloudberry realized. He squealed again, cut off by a bit of water splashing over his face, drowning, and Cloudberry knew she could not leave him.

She swam towards the floundering colt, a flat whinnying sound bursting from her. Panicked, he pawed at her with one good leg, and when she got closer, he put his head on her neck to keep it above the water. She fought against the waves threatening to send them under, snorting with effort. The salty water stung her wounds.

Drake and Nellie ran down to the beach. They saw Cloudberry swimming to the shore, and they called her. She saw them, and continued, too tired to whinny. Waves battered her and her brother as she neared the land. A big one knocked her over as her hooves touched the sand on the bottom of the ocean. Nightcloud fell away from her and scrambled to the shore on three legs, seeming only half conscious, and collapsed into dry sand.

Cloudberry cantered out of the water, wobbling dangerously, then slowed and walked to Drake and Nellie.

"Are you okay? Did you hit any rocks!?" The white-faced, tense humans felt her all over for injury. No more than a few seconds later, she too collapsed into the sand.

"I didn't hit any rocks or anything," she gasped. "What… what happened to Nightcloud?"

Nellie looked over quickly at the black form in the sand. "He's lying over there," she said.

Cloudberry picked herself up with plenty of effort and

walked over warily to the fallen stallion. He lay in the sand gasping for breath, eyes closed, probably unconscious. Cloudberry saw what had been the cracking noise – the top half of his horn was broken off, unevenly. It was half the length it had been. She arched her neck in surprise. Her eyes looked over the rest of his body, almost expecting to see him crushed in places, but though his ribs showed as he breathed, he wasn't broken.

"Is he a horse now?" asked Nellie, coming up beside her and looking at his horn.

"No. He is a unicorn with a broken horn."

"What was wrong with his leg?"

"Not his leg, he hit his shoulder on a rock, I think. See the big scrape."

She turned around and started walking back towards Drake, who was still standing behind her, looking like he had certainly had the biggest scare he could remember.

It took him a while to talk. "I-I guess we should leave," he said finally. "You fought well." He looked at Nightcloud. "I'd rather not be around when he wakes up back up..."

"I don't think I've seen the last of him, either." warned Cloudberry.

She looked at both of the humans, all her tiredness showing, and yet she still moved sideways for them to mount.

They did have to leave. Rest, no matter how inviting, came later. Drake jumped onto her back, followed by Nellie. Nellie thought differently of Nightcloud. He was more ugly, less beautiful and likely to ever be a friend to anyone. Nevertheless, she still liked him the slightest bit, even though he was evil and nearly gave her a heart attack ten minutes ago... she always liked the evil ones, though. Evil guys on television shows were hotter.

Cloudberry trotted tiredly towards the grass at the end of the beach. She would go home – to where the big woods and the house were, and her friend Alidar, and the sorceress sisters. When she was rested up and healed some, she would race again. She didn't think she would have to worry about Nightcloud until he healed. Maybe, if she was lucky, he would not bother her again, or he would suddenly have a change of heart... yeah, right.

They left the beach and the tired stallion behind, Cloudberry trotting along strongly though she was exhausted and bloody where she had been bitten and scraped. Everyone was quiet. Drake patted her neck.

"Do you want to fly?" he asked quietly.

"...Sure." Cloudberry replied.

She flapped out her pearly wings, the humans sliding

back, and began to fly upward slowly, and then descend in a slow glide.

"So, what are we going to do tomorrow... or in the days that come?" Drake asked, wondering.

"I'm going to be a racehorse."

Drake patted her softly and said "That's the kind of spirit I dreamed about." Cloudberry arched her neck and flew upwards again, and Drake, Nellie, and the white filly soon disappeared into the green and blue.

THE END

Glossary of Odd things

Uni: Land of unicorns, dragons, etc., quite similar to earth. It is not a planet, but many places in the universe tied together by gates.

The gates: Gates to other worlds/sections of Uni. Guarded by Galaxy Dancer. Used when beings want to go to Unicorabia, the great beaches, etc.

Noopie: A Qupdoodle, little magical flying seahorse-like thing. He is not exactly the star of the book... YET!!!!! MuahHAhaHAha HAAAA (etc.)

Mammatus: Mammatus is a sort of cloud formation, formed on the underside of storm clouds by sinking air. It looks like pouches dripping off of the bottom of the cloud. Oh yes, and Cloudberry's mom is named after this. Aren't I clever.

Nightcloud: Cloudberry's brother. Sorry, Nightcloud, but you haven't made it out of the glossary yet, so you're still just an object. There will be much more of 'Dr. Drama' in the next book.

Smoke shadow: Famous Uni racehorse. Gray.

Will O The Wisp: Great earth racehorse. I had a name difficulty moment. Sorry.

Feathers: In case you didn't know, feathers are longish hairs around the hoof, pastern and fetlock. Clydesdales, Friesians, cobs and fluffy ponies are some of the horses they can be thick on. Note: Nightcloud does not have giant Clydesdale hooves. (Only in his dreams.)

Stalactites/stalagmites: cave formations formed by the dripping of water from the ceiling of a cave. They stick out like a sore thumb and are very pointy.

Alea Bushardt finished Cloud Filly soon after she turned 14. She is shown here with her Quarter Horse gelding, Sunridge, who can actually write better than her. Unfortunately he can't figure out how to work the keyboard, so he must settle for helping to edit instead (which he is also very good at). Alea enjoys writing, horses, music, hairdos that look like mushrooms, and tall socks. Also some other assorted things.

ISBN 141205429-X